U0132409

TANG AND SONG LYRICS
IN ORIGINAL RHYME

原韻英譯唐宋詞選

Translated by C. K. Ho

何中堅 譯

商務印書館

Tang and Song Lyrics in Original Rhyme
原韻英譯唐宋詞選

選譯：何中堅
Selected and translated by：C. K. Ho
責任編輯：黃家麗
Executive Editor：K. L. Wong
出版：商務印書館（香港）有限公司
Published by：The Commercial Press (H.K.) Limited
香港筲箕灣耀興道3號東滙廣場8樓
8/F, Eastern Central Plaza,
3 Yiu Hing Road, Shau Kei Wan, Hong Kong
http://www.commercialpress.com.hk

發行：香港聯合書刊物流有限公司
Distributed by：The SUP Publishing Logistics (H.K.) Limited
香港新界大埔汀麗路36號中華商務印刷大廈3字樓
3/F, C&C Building, 36 Ting Lai Road,
Tai Po, N. T., Hong Kong

印刷：中華商務彩色印刷有限公司
Printed by：C&C Offset Printing Co., Ltd.
香港新界大埔汀麗路 36 號中華商務印刷大廈 14 字樓
14/F, C&C Building, 36 Ting Lai Road,
Tai Po, N. T., Hong Kong

版次：2018 年 10 月第 1 版第 1 次印刷
Edition：First Edition, First Printing, October 2018
© 2018 商務印書館（香港）有限公司
ISBN 978 962 07 0533 5

獻給我的母親陳淑佳
Dedicated to My Mother Chan Sook Kai

樹欲靜而風不息。　　　　子欲養而親不在。
A tree wants peace,　　　*A son wants to repay,*
But the wind won't cease.　*But his parents won't stay.*

Contents
目 錄

TANG AND SONG LYRICS 唐宋詞

Preface

This is a long-awaited sequel to the author's previous book, *Tang Poems in Original Rhyme*, which was published three years ago. In this exciting new book, the author extends his Ho Translation Style to re-create 101 Tang and Song ci-poems / lyrics (唐宋詞) in English. The ci-poems are ancient Chinese melodic lyrics of songs. The structure and form of ci-poems are much more complicated than those of Tang poems, which makes the task of creating this volume much more difficult than that of the previous book by the author.

It is already an enormous task to translate one ci-poem in a way that does not only preserve its rhyme and melodic flavour, but also faithfully conveys the emotions and feelings of the original author in simple English. To translate 101 ci-poems using the Ho Translation Style is not possible without a deep understanding of Chinese literature, excellent proficiency in English, and, most importantly, passion. The author's passion for ancient Chinese poetry urged him to show the English-speaking world the beauty of Chinese poems by translating them in the Ho Translation Style. He has done this magnificently for the Tang poems in his previous book and, even more magnificently, for the ci-poems in this book.

Same as in the previous book, the translations are supplemented with many footnotes that help readers understand the background and story behind each ci-poem. To readers who are not familiar with ancient Chinese literature, the footnotes are essential for them to appreciate the beauty of the ci-poems and comprehend the emotions and feelings of their authors. Each translated ci-poem shows the author's ingenious use of words and in-depth knowledge of ancient Chinese literature.

In addition to presenting the exquisiteness of ci-poems to English speakers, this book provides another angle for English-speaking, bilingual Chinese to appreciate ci-poems and, therefore, arouse their interest in ancient Chinese literature. For Chinese speakers, it is a fun and interesting way to learn English by reading this book. If you have read the author's previous book, you should not miss this one. Whatever your expectations are, you will not be disappointed. If you have not read the author's previous book, you will want to rush to buy it after reading this one.

Professor Chau Kwong-wing
The University of Hong Kong

前言

　　本書是繼三年前《原韻英譯唐詩精選》出版後，讀者期待已久的「原韻英譯中國古典詩詞系列」內又一佳作。本書精彩之處在於譯者繼成功翻譯唐詩之後，以同一創新、獨特翻譯手法，用簡淺英語重新塑造 101 首唐宋詞，並保留其韻律及音樂感。（在上一本書的前言，我稱此種手法為"何氏翻譯風格"）。唐宋詞的結構與格式比較唐詩複雜，因而其翻譯難度亦因此較譯者以前一本書為高。

　　將一首詞翻譯為英語而要保留其韻律及音樂感，並且要把古代詩人的感情及思想如實表達，本身就是一件異常艱鉅的工作。若非在中國文學上有相當造詣、精通英語並且有一份激情，根本不可能以此種手法譯出 101 首唐宋詞。譯者這份激情最為重要，足以驅使他完成這件艱辛工作，向英語讀者展示中國詩詞的美。在他以前的兩本書裏，讀者已經看到了他非凡的翻譯功夫。在此本書裏，他的翻譯功夫更為卓越。

　　跟以前的譯本一樣，許多詞的下面都加了腳注，以幫助不熟悉中國古典文學的讀者了解詞人或詩人的背景或歷史。這些註腳對欣賞詞的意境及領悟詞人的思想和感情至為重要。譯本中每首詞皆顯現出譯者運用英語的巧妙手法，及其對中國古典文學的高深造詣。

　　此英譯本除了向英語讀者展示唐宋詞的美之外，亦可以讓通曉中英語的華人從另一個角度欣賞詞，從而引起他們對中國古典文學的興趣。對其他華人來說，閱讀此英譯本亦是學習英語饒富樂趣的途徑。假如你已經看過譯者的前一本書，你不應該錯過這一本。因為無論你的要求有多高，這本書都不會令你失望。假如你不曾看過譯者的書的話，當你看了這本書之後，定必會急不及待去買譯者的前一本。

鄒廣榮教授

香港大學

Preface

Translating Chinese *ci*-poetry into English is not an easy task. The translator has to be well versed in traditional Chinese poetry, in particular the styles of the selected *ci*-poets, and proficient in English so as to be able to bring out the flavour and spirit of the original works in the most readable manner for the appreciation of the English-reading public.

Some scholars question the translatability of poetry, and also *ci*-poetry for that matter. They hold the view that poetry is a kind of writing which is not translatable. According to Jackson Matthews, "to translate a poem whole is to compose another poem". Robert Frost also makes the famous statement that "poetry is what gets lost in translation". Other scholars, however, believe that what is said in one language can be conveyed in another language, including the poetic language. Andre Lefevere, for example, proposed seven strategies for translating poetry in his book *Translating Poetry: Seven Strategies and a Blueprint* (1975). One of the methods he proposed is rhymed translation, which is to rhyme the translation according to the schemes of the target language to create the poetic flavour. The use of rhyme, in the view of John Turner, who translated *A Golden Treasury of Chinese Poetry*, is "to make the translation of a poem to read like a poem itself", and "to preserve the singing or musical quality in Chinese". It is generally agreed that a *ci*-poem is a song without music. Rhyming is thus an important part of a song and a lyric.

This book, *Tang and Song Lyrics in Original Rhyme*, sets out to render the literary and musical features of *ci*-poetry in the best possible manner. Mr C.K. Ho, by vocation a surveyor and by avocation a seasoned literary translator, has shown us how beautiful lyrics in Chinese could be turned into English in a way that is a feast for both the ears and for the eyes.

Professor Chan Sin-wai
School of Humanities (Translation Programme)
The Chinese University of Hong Kong, Shenzhen

前言

　　將中國詞翻譯成英語並不是一件容易的事情。譯者必須對中國古典詩詞 — 特別是所選唐宋詞人的詞風 — 有深厚造詣並且精通英語，才可以用地道的英語將原詞的韻味神髓翻譯出來供英語讀者欣賞。

　　有些學者質疑詩詞的可譯性，認為詩是一種不能翻譯的文體。美國詩人及翻譯家傑克遜‧馬修斯說：「完整翻譯一首詩等如創作另一首詩」。另一位美國詩人羅伯特‧佛洛斯特亦有句名言：「詩就是翻譯中失去的東西」。不過，亦有一些學者相信，能夠以一種語言表達的 — 包括詩 — 都能夠以另外一種語言來表達。例如，翻譯理論學者安德烈‧勒弗 爾在其一九七五年出版的著作《詩歌翻譯：七種策略和一個藍圖》中倡議採用七種策略去翻譯詩，而其中一種策略就是押韻翻譯。即是按譯入語的韻律押韻，以期在譯文中重塑詩的韻味。翻譯家唐安石在譯作《英譯中詩金庫》中認為押韻翻譯「讓譯出來的詩唸起來像首詩」，並且「能保留中文原詩的唱歌感或音樂感」。眾所周知，詞是無樂之歌，韻律因而是歌和詞的重要部份。

　　《原韻英譯唐宋詞選》旨在以最巧妙的方法譯出唐宋詞的美文美韻。何中堅先生是一位執業測量師及經驗豐富的業餘文學翻譯者，他的譯本讓我們看到美麗的唐宋詞如何轉化為悅耳、悅目的英語詩篇。

陳善偉教授
香港中文大學（深圳）人文社科學院翻譯系

Translator's Preface

Poems of Tang dynasty (唐詩) and lyrics of Tang and Song dynasties (唐宋詞) are precious literary legacies left by great ancient Chinese poets. They have been popular among the Chinese people all over the world for over one thousand years and have profound influence on Chinese culture. Many of these masterpieces contain phrases that have since become proverbial in the Chinese language.

This book contains my translation of 101 Tang and Song lyrics and it is the second book in a series of books on rhymed translation of classical Chinese poetry. My first book in this series entitled *Tang Poems in Original Rhyme* was published in 2015.

An innovative approach was adopted to reproduce these 101 famous lyrics in English by preserving their compelling qualities while faithfully recreating the text. The translations in this book are unique in that they are succinct, faithful to and rhyme in the same way as the originals. My aim is to make the translated versions elegant and melodious like the originals. I sincerely hope that the beauty and soul of the lyrics are also recreated and that they would read like poems themselves. Simple English is used to ensure pleasant reading.

I was prompted to embark on this innovative translation work by my love for Chinese literature and my desire to show to the world, especially to the younger generation, the beauty of classical Chinese literature so as to popularize traditional Chinese culture.

Nowadays, our younger generation has a relatively good command of the English language. For those who have a taste for literature, I believe a version of lyrics in simple, easy-to-understand English may attract them to classical Chinese literature. They may otherwise be put off by difficult classical Chinese words and phrases, especially when allegories and metaphors are present. To help readers to better understand and appreciate the lyrics, footnotes are included after some lyrics to explain a legend, an allusion, a metaphor, a place, a custom, or the background.

My love for classical Chinese literature is partly inherited from my mother and partly nurtured. My mother had a strong love for classical Chinese literature. She taught me how to appreciate classical prose and poems and how to read and recite them when I was a little boy. I was not old enough to fully understand the contents but I remember I was deeply touched by the stories behind. Today, thanks to my beloved mother, I can still recite a few pretty long proses and poems which had long since been engraved in my mind.

The lyrics in this book were selected from popular and representative works of 36 great poets of Tang and Song dynasties. Among these, some record the poets' powerful feelings aroused by circumstances, often with a hidden message; some grieve over parting from their loved ones or homeland; some lament the loss of their country or territories, pouring out strong passion as patriots. Examples are: Li Yu's 'Fair Lady Yu' (虞美人), Liu Yung's 'Bells in the Rain' (雨霖鈴) and Yue Fei's 'The River Runs Red' (滿江紅).

Owing to the enormous differences between the two languages and the cultures of the two peoples, translating classical Chinese poems / lyrics into English is a complex, difficult and challenging task. One would note that not all words and phrases in Chinese that touch one's heart have suitable equivalents in English.

To ensure genuine re-creation of the lyrics in English, the translator has to immerse himself in the lyrics and to come up with words and lines that aptly set the scenes and describe the delicate emotions as if he is writing lyrics of his own. Over the past three years, I spent all my free time in researching the background of lyrics and recapturing the thoughts and emotions of ancient poets. The most difficult part of the translation was in the choice of words and phrases that serve the purpose while at the same time preserving the rhyme, rhythm and flavour of the lyrics.

Often, the same rhyme repeats many times (sometimes up to ten times) in lyrics. Identifying suitable rhyming words posed great difficulties. This is because there are much fewer suitable rhyming words in the English language compared with the Chinese language. There were many unsuccessful attempts. Translations were revised many times and some were abandoned. The work was demanding and required dedication, courage, and perseverance. Under no circumstances, however, had I twisted or sacrificed the original meaning of a line for the sake of rhyme matching.

As a separate literary genre, quite distinct from Tang poems, lyrics originated in the middle to late Tang dynasty (A.D. 618 – A.D. 907). They took a different, much more refined and enriched form and continued to develop reaching its apex in Song dynasty (A.D. 960 – A.D. 1279) before gradually declining in the early days of Yuen dynasty (A.D. 1279 – A.D. 1368).

This form of poetry was originally written for singing and was set to local or foreign (barbarian) folk music (mostly from Central and Western Asia and some from places such as India and Myanmar). Indeed, the popular tune pattern 'Heavenly Barbarian' (菩薩蠻) was from a Burmese song which praised the hair-dresses of a Burmese empress.

Each lyric was set to one of the melodies or so-called tune patterns (詞牌) bearing a specific title. In so doing, the characters used in the lyric had to match the tone and rhythm of the tune besides rhyming. In order to fit the words into melodies, lyrics were therefore often made up of long and short lines with varied rhymes and beats. They are therefore markedly different from and certainly more melodious than Tang poems. There were over one thousand tune patterns in use in Song dynasty of which about two hundred were popular.

Lyrics were well-received and became popular among intellectuals, officials, and nobilities partly because they expressed subtle feelings more effectively and partly because listeners were fascinated and thrilled by the music, especially the vibrant Central and Western Asian music. They were therefore often sung at banquets and pleasure houses.

It should be noted that the titles of lyrics are in fact the titles of tune patterns which bear no relation to the contents of the lyrics. Over time, most of the tunes were lost but lyrics continued to be written to the tune patterns. As such, lyrics became a separate form of poetry occupying an important place in Chinese literature.

The following are two examples of rhyme and rhythm matching:

(1) Crows Cawing at Night by Li Yu

Alone and wordless,
    *up the western tower I **go**;*
*The moon's like a **bow**.*

Lonely is the Wutong in the gloomy courtyard
    *shrouded in the bleakness of autumn **below**.*

*Cutting cannot **sever**;*
*Handling it but it remains tangled as **ever**....*

*It is separation **woe**:*
*Feelings like no other, in my heart **overflow**!*

(1) 烏夜啼—李煜

無言獨上西**樓**，月如**鈎**。
寂寞梧桐深院鎖清**秋**。

剪不**斷**，理還**亂**，
是離**愁**，
別是一番滋味在心**頭**。

(2) Eternal Longing by Ouyang Xiu

*Flowers are like **you**,*
*Willows are like **you**.*

Flowers and willows were young
*when we bade each other **adieu**.*
*Bowing your head, tears you burst **into**.*

East of the Yangtze River,
*West of it **too**.*

On both shores,
*separately mandarin ducks **flew**.*
*As to when they'll meet again none has a **clue**.*

(2) 長相思—歐陽修

花似**伊**，柳似**伊**，
花柳青春人別**離**。
低頭雙淚**垂**。

長江東，長江**西**，
兩岸鴛鴦兩處**飛**。
相逢知幾**時**。

My heart-felt thanks are due to Professor K. W. Chau of The University of Hong Kong and Professor Chan Sin-wai of The Chinese University of Hong Kong, Shenzhen for the prefaces of this book which they so kindly took time out of their busy schedules to write.

My heart-felt thanks are also due to my colleagues and friends at The University of Hong Kong for their support of my work especially to Mr H. F. Leung. Very special thanks are due to C. T. who patiently and critically read the entire manuscript and gave me invaluable opinions and suggestions continuously over the long years.

Lastly, I would like to express my profound gratitude to Miss Betty K. L. Wong of The Commercial Press (HK) Ltd. for her advice and excellent editorial work during the preparation of this volume.

C. K. Ho

譯者前言

　　唐詩與唐宋詞是唐朝及宋朝無數偉大詩人詞人流傳下來的珍貴文化遺產，傳誦於國內及海外華人社會千餘年，對中華文化影響深遠。其中很多是家傳戶曉的偉大作品。詩詞內亦有不少大家耳熟能詳的名句和成語。

　　本書精選 101 首英譯唐宋詞，是"原韻英譯中國古典詩詞"系列內的第二個譯本。第一本《原韻英譯唐詩精選》，已於 2015 年出版。

　　本人採用創新手法，以英語重塑 101 首著名唐宋詞。既保留其優美動人的特質，又忠實譯出其原意。此英譯本獨特之處，在於跟原詞一樣簡潔及以同樣方式押韻，意欲令英譯本如同原詞一樣優美及富音樂感。本人懇切希望，此英譯本能夠將唐宋詞的美與神韻重新塑造出來，及令其唸起來像唸詩一樣。譯本採用簡單英語，以求唸起來流暢自然。

　　我從事此項創新翻譯，是因為我對中國古典文學的熱愛，以及我渴望向全世界 — 特別是年青的一代 — 展示唐宋詞美妙傳神之處，從而推廣傳統中華文化。

　　當今年青的一代英語水平比較高。我相信一本簡淺易明的英語譯本，可能會吸引文學愛好者接觸傳統中國文學。否則，他們會被古典詩詞內艱深的詞語、隱喻及典故嚇怕。為了幫助讀者了解及欣賞唐宋詞，我在一些詞下面加上腳注，來解釋一些典故、隱喻、傳說、風俗、地點及當時的歷史背景等。

　　我對中國古典文學的愛好，一半由於我母親的遺傳，一半是後天培養的。我母親熱愛中國古典文學。從小她就教我唸和背誦古詩文，也教我如何欣賞詩文的內涵。當時年紀小小的我雖然未能完全明白，卻每每為裏面的故事所感動。我後來發現，當日她的教導已經深深烙印在我的腦海裏面。感謝我摯愛的母親，直到今天我仍然可以背出好幾篇頗長的古文、古詩詞。

　　本書內的唐宋詞出自三十六位唐宋時代偉大詩人之手，全部都是傳世佳作。其中有觸景傷情，憑詞寄意；有吐盡離愁，緬懷故人或故國；有慷慨悲歌，抒發愛國熱情。例如：李煜的"虞美人"、柳永的"雨霖鈴"及岳飛的"滿江紅"等。

　　中國人和英國人無論在語言或文化上，都存在巨大差異。因此將古典詩詞翻譯成英語是一項複雜、困難及富於挑戰性的工作。因為並非所有動人心弦的中文詞句，皆有等同的英語詞句。

　　為了要正確無誤地重塑唐宋詞，譯者必須深入鑽研每一首詞，從而找出最貼切的英語，來描述當時的情景、意境及細膩的感情，就好像自己在作詞一樣。在過去的三年裏面，我努力考究這些詞的背景，及捕捉古代詞人的思想與感情。在翻譯過程中，最困難的地方在於選取合適的字詞和句子，而這些字詞和句子，必須要同時能夠保留原作品的韻律、節奏及神髓。

　　唐宋詞的腳韻經常會多次重複（有時候重複多達十次），因此，要挑選多個合適的同音字來配腳韻十分困難。因為在英語裏面，可以用的同音字遠遠比中文的少。很多時候，因為找不到到合適的字詞或句子而翻譯失敗，要從頭再做多次甚至放棄整篇草稿。翻譯過程相當艱鉅，需要高度專注力、勇氣及堅毅力。雖然如此，在任何情況下，我從來沒有為了配腳韻而犧牲或扭曲原詞句的含義。

　　詞與唐詩是兩種截然不同的文體。詞起源於中唐至晚唐（公元 618–907），以嶄新及更豐富的形式不斷發展，至宋朝（公元 960–1279）臻完美。及至元朝（公元 1279–1368）初則逐漸式微。

　　詞，又稱曲子詞，本來是為本地及外地（中西亞或稱蠻族、或印度、緬甸）民歌所配的曲詞。當時其中有一個流行的詞牌叫"菩薩蠻"，其樂譜就是出自緬甸一首歌頌緬甸女皇頭飾的歌曲。

　　作詞（傳統上稱為填詞）的時候，詩人將句子配到一首固定樂譜上。而所根據的樂曲則稱為"詞牌"。每一個"詞牌"皆按其原樂曲冠上名字。

為了要配合原樂曲的旋律、韻律與節奏，填詞人選詞用字必須與“詞牌”吻合。因而往往要採用長短句及多變化的韻律。因此，它與傳統唐詩有明顯不同之處，也更富音樂感。在宋朝時期，通用的“詞牌”有逾千個，流行的約有二百個。

詞在當時廣受文人雅士和達官貴人喜愛。其中一個原因，是它能夠強而有力地表達細膩的感情，加上詞所配的音樂 (特別是中西亞或稱蠻族的鏗鏘音樂) 令聽曲者着迷，因此詞經常在宴會上及歡樂場所中配以音樂唱出來以娛樂賓客。

有一點值得注意的是，一首詞的名字，其實是“詞牌”的名字 (亦即是原來樂曲的名字)，與詞的內容完全沒有關連。隨着年代消逝，大部份樂譜已經不復存在。不過，愛好填詞的人，仍舊繼續按照“詞牌”填詞。自此，詞就成為另一種體裁，在中國文學上有其重要的位置。

以下是兩則用英語配韻及節奏的例子：

(1) 烏夜啼 — 李煜

> 無言獨上西**樓**，月如**鈎**。
> 寂寞梧桐深院鎖清**秋**。
>
> 剪不**斷**，理還**亂**，
> 　　是離**愁**，
> 別是一番滋味在心**頭**。

(1) Crows Cawing at Night by Li Yu

> *Alone and wordless,*
> 　　*up the western tower I **go**;*
> *The moon's like a **bow**.*
>
> *Lonely is the Wutong in the gloomy courtyard*
> 　　*shrouded in the bleakness of autumn **below**.*

*Cutting cannot **sever**;*
*Handing it but it remains tangled as **ever**….*

*It is separation **woe**:*
*Feelings like no other, in my heart **overflow**!*

(2) 長相思 — 歐陽修

花似**伊**，柳似**伊**，
花柳青春人別**離**。
低頭雙淚**垂**。

長江東，長江**西**，
兩岸鴛鴦兩處**飛**。
相逢知幾**時**。

(2) Eternal Longing by Ouyang Xiu

*Flowers are like **you**,*
*Willows are like **you**.*

Flowers and willows were young
*when we bade each other **adieu**.*
*Bowing your head, tears you burst **into**.*

East of the Yangtze River,
*West of it **too**.*

On both shores,
*separately mandarin ducks **flew**.*
*As to when they'll meet again none has a **clue**.*

衷心感謝香港大學鄒廣榮教授及香港中文大學（深圳）陳善偉教授，他們兩位在百忙之中抽出寶貴時間為此書寫前言。

同時亦要感謝香港大學的同事及友好，尤其是梁慶豐先生給我的支持。另外，特別要感謝 C.T. 這些年來耐心和認真地審閱全部文稿，並提出不少寶貴意見。

最後，衷心感謝香港商務印書館的黃家麗小姐在籌備本書當中，給予指點、協助，及其精湛的編輯技巧。

何中堅

TANG AND SONG LYRICS
唐宋詞

A FISHERMAN'S SONG

Zhang Zhihe (? — 744)

In front of Xisai Mountain[1], egrets fly;
Blooming are the peach trees,
    fat the *gui fish*[2] in the water running by.

Wearing blue bamboo hat
    and green straw cape,
Home I needn't go –
    slanting wind and drizzles I defy.

1 A mountain in Wuxing county (吳興縣) in Zhejiang Province.
2 A kind of fish (即桂魚) commonly found in rivers in Zhejiang Province.

漁歌子

張志和 (? — 744)

西塞山前白鷺飛，
桃花流水鱖魚肥。

青箬笠，綠蓑衣。
斜風細雨不須歸。

NOT A FLOWER, NOR MIST

Bai Juyi (772 — 846)

Like a flower but it isn't;
Like mist but it isn't.

It comes in the middle of the night;
It goes at break of dawn.

Like a spring dream, it comes,
    but never stays long;
Like morning clouds, it goes,
    and can't be found once gone.

Note:
It is not known what the poet was referring to in this lyric poem. In ancient times, however, the phrases 'spring dream' and 'morning clouds' were often used to allude to secret meetings of lovers. It is therefore believed that the poet was referring to some deeply memorable romantic encounters.

花非花

白居易 (772 — 846)

花非花，霧非霧。
夜半來，天明去。

來如春夢不多時，
去似朝雲無覓處。

HEAVENLY BARBARIAN

Anonymous Song from Dun Huang (5ᵗʰ to 10ᵗʰ century)

On my pillow, a thousand vows you've made:
You won't divorce me
　　till the green mountains have decayed;

Till the steelyard weight floats on water-top,
And the Yellow River completely dries up;

Till the stars, Orion and Lucifer,
　　appear together in broad daylight[1],
And the Big Dipper[2] seen in the south at night.

So, divorce me you cannot,
Till the sun at midnight we spot.

1 These two stars (參辰二星) are positioned respectively in the west and east. Hence, they never appear together in the night sky, not to mention appearing together in broad daylight.

2 The Plough or Northern Stars.

菩薩蠻

敦煌曲子詞（五至十世紀 — 無名氏）

枕前發盡千般願：要休且待青山爛。
水面上秤錘浮，直待黃河徹底枯。

白日參辰現，北斗回南面。
休即未能休，且待三更見日頭。

Background:
This and the following lyric poem by anonymous poets of the Song Dynasty were selected from about 1,300 songs / poems among some 30,000 to 40,000 ancient texts hidden in a secret cache inside a sealed cave temple in Dun Huang (敦煌). The cache was accidentally found by a Daoist in 1900.

VIEWING THE RIVER SOUTH

Anonymous Song from Dun Huang (5th to 10th century)

The moon hangs in the sky,
Like a lump of silver in a distant sight.

The wind's rising in the deep of the night.
Pray blow away the clouds
    surrounding the moon outright,

So that my ungrateful lover would be in sight.

望江南

敦煌曲子詞（五至十世紀 ─ 無名氏）

天上月，遙望似一團銀。

夜久更闌風漸緊。與奴吹散月邊雲。
照見負心人。

WATER CLOCK (1)

Wen Tingyun (812 — 870)

Incense from the jade censer rises,
Tears[1] down the red candles fall,
Evoking sad feelings in a painted hall.

Her eyebrow make-up faded,
Her hair untidy.
In the long night, the quilt and pillow grow icy.

1   Melted wax-drops falling from a burning candle were likened to teardrops falling down from a person's face.

Pattering on the Wutong tree
Is the midnight rain,
That has no regard for her parting pain.

From leaf to leaf, it falls,
Drop by drop – the drip goes on,
Landing on the empty steps till dawn.

更漏子 (1)

温庭筠 (812 — 870)

玉鑪香，紅蠟淚，
　偏照畫堂秋思。

眉翠薄，鬢雲殘，
　夜長衾枕寒。

梧桐樹，三更雨，
　不道離情正苦。

一葉葉，一聲聲，
　空階滴到明。

WATER CLOCK (2)

Wen Tingyun (812 — 870)

Stars are sparse;
Tolls and drumbeats[1] die.
Outside the curtain
    under a fading moon, orioles cry.

Dews on orchids are thick;
In the wind, willows sway.
Fallen flowers heap up in the yard in disarray.

In the empty attic,
Over the balustrade, she gives a stare:
Like last year, sadness fills the air.

---

1   Tolls and drumbeats came from the watch tower to signal time at night in ancient times. These ceased when dawn approached.

Spring's waning,
Endless thoughts in her mind gleam:
Bygone joys are like a dream.

更漏子 (2)

温庭筠 (812 — 870)

星斗稀，鐘鼓歇，
簾外鶯啼殘月。

蘭露重，柳風斜，
滿庭堆落花。

虛閣上，倚闌望，
還似去年惆悵。

春欲暮，思無窮，
舊歡如夢中。

WATER CLOCK (3)

Wen Tingyun (812 — 870)

Willow threads are long;
Spring rain drizzles.
Beyond the flowers,
     the distant water clock dribbles.

Border wild geese are startled,
So are the city crows.
A golden partridge
     on the painted screen glows.

The fragrant smoke's thin:
It penetrates the curtain and the screen –
The Xie's[1] pool and pavilion is a sad scene.

The red candle's shaded;
The embroidered curtain hangs low:
Endlessly I dream, but you'd never know.

---

1 Originally, it was the family name of a famous singing girl. Later, this was used generally to indicate the home of a lady.

更漏子 (3)

温庭筠 (812 — 870)

柳絲長，春雨細，
花外漏聲迢遞。
驚塞雁，起城烏，畫屏金鷓鴣。

香霧薄，透簾幕，
惆悵謝家池閣。
紅燭背，繡簾垂，夢長君不知。

HEAVENLY BARBARIAN (1)

Wen Tingyun (812 — 870)

Inside the moonlit ornate tower,
　　ceaselessly for you I pine;
Spring's saying goodbye to the
　　the delicate and slender willow line.

Outside the door,
　　the grass was thick and green;
I heard the horse neigh
　　when off you were seen.

On the silk curtain,
　　kingfishers were embroidered in gold;
Down a perfumed candle, wax tears rolled[1].

Outside the green window,
　　flowers fall and cuckoos call:
Shattering my dreams, hopes and all.

1　Melted wax-drops falling from a burning candle were likened to teardrops that fell down her
　face after parting from her lover.

菩薩蠻 (1)

温庭筠 (812 — 870)

玉樓明月長相憶，柳絲裊娜春無力。
門外草萋萋，送君聞馬嘶。

畫羅金翡翠，香燭銷成淚。
花落子規啼，綠窗殘夢迷。

Background:
This poem describes a lady inside a tower feeling sad in late spring pining for her lover and recalling the time of parting.

HEAVENLY BARBARIAN (2)

Wen Tingyun (812 — 870)

Grass pillows lie behind crystal screens:
Warm, perfumed
    mandarin-duck brocade induces dreams.

With misty willows the riverside's strewn;
Wild geese fly across the sky under a fading moon.

Dressed in purplish white[1],
Her hair is bedecked with
    effigies cut to varying height[2].

Sweet flowers adorn her temples;
A jade hairpin on her head in the wind trembles.

1 The colour of lotus root fibres is purplish white which was also the colour of the autumn
   season in ancient China.

2 As an ancient custom, women adorned their hair with paper effigies in bright colours on the
   seventh day after the Lunar New Year. This day is also known as "everybody's birthday" (人
   日) and is still being observed today.

Background:
This poem describes a lady dressing up in the morning in her boudoir on the seventh day after
the Lunar New Year.

菩薩蠻 (2)

温庭筠 (812 — 870)

水精簾裏頗黎枕，暖香惹夢鴛鴦錦。
江上柳如煙，雁飛殘月天。

藕絲秋色淺，人勝參差剪。
雙鬢隔香紅，玉釵頭上風。

HEAVENLY BARBARIAN (3)

Wen Tingyun (812 — 870)

On layers of small hills,
    the sun casts golden glittering streaks[1];
Fine hair seeks to cross
    her fragrant, snow-white cheeks[2]

She gets up and
    paints her eyebrows at a slow pace;
She sluggishly washes and makes up her face.

To wear a flower,
    mirrors at front and back she aligns;
The flower and her face on each other shines.

On the silk vest she wears,
Are newly embroidered
    golden partridges in pairs.

---

1 The morning sunbeams shone through the window on the small hills painted on a screen
  beside a bed in which a lady was sleeping.

2 As she turned in bed, her loosened hair slowly drifted over her snow-white cheeks.

菩薩蠻 (3)

温庭筠 (812 — 870)

小山重疊金明滅，雲鬢欲渡香腮雪。
懶起畫娥眉，弄妝梳洗遲。

照花前後鏡，花面交相映。
新帖繡羅襦，雙雙金鷓鴣。

Background:
This poem describes a lady waking up alone in her boudoir, listless and longing for love. The last two lines are a veiled description of her mind.

DREAMING OF RIVER SOUTH (1)

Wen Tingyun (812 — 870)

Dressing-up done,
Inside the river-view pavilion, she leans alone.

Thousands of sails passed by but not his.
The water gently flows,
    the slanting sun shines with a loving tone.

At Duckweed Isle, sorrowful she has grown.

夢江南 (1)

温庭筠 (812 — 870)

梳洗罷，獨倚望江樓。

過盡千帆皆不是，斜暉脈脈水悠悠。
腸斷白蘋洲。

DREAMING OF RIVER SOUTH (2)

Wen Tingyun (812 — 870)

Thousands and thousands of regrets,
The deepest lies at the end of the sky.

Mountains and the moon
      know not what's in my mind,
Flowers fall in the rain and wind before the eye.

Drifting emerald clouds slantingly lie.

夢江南 (2)

温庭筠 (812 — 870)

千萬恨，恨極在天涯。

山月不知心裏事，水風空落眼前花，
搖曳碧雲斜。

Background:
This poem describes the feelings of a lady who sadly missed her love who had travelled to a faraway place and there was no one to share her sorrows. The last line is a veiled description of the passing of time as the clouds gradually changed position.

A SOUTHERN SONG

Wen Tingyun (812 — 870)

He's got a golden parakeet in his hand,
An embroidered phoenix on his chest.

After a stealthy look,
        secretly I've him assessed.

Just marry him –
To be a pair of lovebirds is best.

南歌子

温庭筠 (812 — 870)

手裏金鸚鵡，胸前繡鳳凰。
偷眼暗形相。

不如從嫁與，作鴛鴦。

WILLOW BRANCHES

Wen Tingyun (812 — 870)

Weaving brocade by the loom,
    orioles again and again call,
Stopping the shuttle in tears,
    the traveller she'd recall.

It's still freezing cold in the frontier
    in the third month,
Though there're willows,
    he won't notice spring's come at all.

Background:
This poem describes a wife weaving brocade by the loom in spring. The calls of orioles reminded her of her soldier husband who was stationed in the freezing cold frontier in the far north.

楊柳枝

温庭筠 (812 — 870)

織錦機邊鶯語頻，
停梭垂淚憶征人。

塞門三月猶蕭索，
縱有垂楊未覺春。

FAIR LADY YU

Li Yu (937 — 978)

When will spring flowers and
    the autumn moon be gone?
How much do I know of things bygone?

To the small chamber,
    again came the east wind last night;
How unbearable to recall
    my lost kingdom in the moonlight!

They should still be there,
    the jade steps and carved rail, [1]
But rosy cheeks have turned pale. [2]

Do you know how much sorrow there is?
Just like a river of spring flowing east!

1 The palace structure.
2 The rosy cheeks of young palace ladies. Here the poet meant all good and beautiful things in
   his palace had changed.

虞美人

李煜 (937 — 978)

春花秋月何時了？
往事知多少？

小樓昨夜又東風，
故國不堪回首月明中。

雕闌玉砌應猶在，
只是朱顏改。

問君能有幾多愁？
恰似一江春水向東流！

Background:
The poet Li Yu was the last king of the Southern Tang Dynasty (南唐) which he ruled from
A.D. 961-975. He was overthrown by the Song Emperor, Song Tai Zu, Zhao Kuangyin (宋太
祖趙匡胤 927-976). Upon surrender, he was taken to Bianjing (汴京), the capital of Song,
and kept under house arrest as a prisoner. He was granted death by poison three years later on
the seventh day of the seventh month in A.D. 978 at the age of 42, not long after he composed
this lyric which was believed to have upset the Song Emperor. He composed this and many
other touching lyrics during the three years in captivity, as he could not cast away the memories
of his lost kingdom. He wished there were no more flowers and silvery moon to remind him
of the happy days in his own palace.

CROWS CAWING AT NIGHT (1)

Li Yu (937 — 978)

Flowers in the woods wither as
    the splendour of spring fades:
What a great haste!

Chilly rains in the morn and
    winds at night one often hates.

Rouged tears[1] you shed,
Made me drunk and fascinated.

When can I return who knows? [2]
Life's forever beset with regrets
    as water forever eastward flows.

1 The poet watched flowers fall from trees in the rain and likened them to rouged tears (i.e. tears mixed with rouge) falling on a woman's face. Rouge is a red cosmetic powder used by women as make-up in the old days. He recalled his queen shedding tears when they were taken away from their palace.

2 Return to his palace. The poet was sighing for a lost kingdom. He did not know when he could return to his palace.

烏夜啼 (1)

李煜 (937 — 978)

林花榭了春紅，太匆匆。
常恨朝來寒雨晚來風。

胭脂淚，留人醉。
幾時重？
自是人生長恨水長東。

Background:
The poet likened the close of spring season to the end of his reign. He knew he could never regain his kingdom. It was like a river running east that would never return.

CROWS CAWING AT NIGHT (2)

Li Yu (937 — 978)

Alone and wordless,
      up the western tower I go;
The moon's like a bow.

Lonely is the Wutong[1] in the gloomy courtyard
      shrouded in the bleakness of autumn below.

Cutting cannot sever;
Handling it but it remains tangled as ever....

It is separation woe:
Feelings like no other, in my heart overflow!

---

1 Wutong tree.

Background:
Upon surrender to the Song Emperor, the poet was taken to Bianjing (汴京), the capital of Song, and kept under house arrest for three years. The loss of his kingdom filled his mind with extreme grief and inexpressible, bitter feelings.

烏夜啼 (2)

李煜 (937 — 978)

無言獨上西樓，月如鉤。
寂寞梧桐深院鎖清秋。

剪不斷，理還亂，
是離愁，
別是一番滋味在心頭。

WAVES WASHING SANDS (1)

Li Yu (937 — 978)

Outside the curtain, the rain's murmuring:
Waning is the mood of spring.

Too thin is the silk quilt
    to withstand dawn's cold sting.

Not knowing being a captive in my dreams,
I indulge in the momentary joys they bring.

Never should one
    alone by the balustrade stand!¹

Boundless is my land;
Easy it was to part but returning is banned².

Gone is spring
    with the running water and fallen blossoms:
In Heaven and among men.³

---

1 The poet was worried that a distant view from the balcony would remind him of his lost
    kingdom.
2 He was not allowed to return to his palace and he knew he could never regain his kingdom.
3 Emperors and kings in ancient China considered themselves to be Sons of Heaven (天子).
    He had lost everything: in Heaven and among men.

Background:
This is known to be the last lyric poem written by the poet before he was granted death by
poisoning by the Song Emperor, (宋太宗) on the seventh day of the seventh month in A.D.
978 at the age of 42.

浪淘沙 (1)

李煜 (937 — 978)

簾外雨潺潺，春意闌珊。
羅衾不耐五更寒。
夢裏不知身是客，一晌貪歡。

獨自莫憑闌！
無限江山，別時容易見時難。
流水落花春去也，天上人間！

WAVES WASHING SANDS (2)

Li Yu (937 — 978)

One can only lament what had gone by!
No relief is found from scenes before the eye.

Autumn wind blows in the yard –
    the steps the mosses occupy[1].

The beaded curtains hang idly unrolled[1] –
All day long who'd come by?

Sunk and buried,
    in the river-bed the golden chains[2] lie;
Among wild grasses, all ambitions[3] die.

The night's cool,
    the moon shines bright in the clear sky,

I can visualize the jade towers of my palace,
Emptily reflected in the waters of the Qinhuai[4].

1 The steps were occupied by mosses; the door curtain was hanging low and not rolled up. As
 a prisoner being kept in house arrest, he had very few visitors.

2 The story of the defeat of Wu's (吳國) troops in the Three Kingdoms Period (A.D. 220-
 280). Wu blockaded the Yangtze River with large iron chains to stop the fleet of the invading
 Jin (晉國) troops. The Jins burnt and broke the chains which sank into the riverbed. The
 King of Wu was taken prisoner. The poet used this story to allude to his own situation.

3 After being overthrown by the Song Emperor, all his ambitions were gone.

4 The Qinhuai River (秦淮河), a tributary of the Yangtze River that runs past the city of
 Nanjing (南京), the capital of Southern Tang (南唐).

浪淘沙 (2)

李煜 (937 — 978)

往事只堪哀！對景難排。

秋風庭院蘚侵階。

一行珠簾閒不捲，終日誰來？

金鎖已沉埋，壯氣蒿萊。

晚涼天淨月華開。

想得玉樓瑤殿影，空照秦淮。

BREAKING THROUGH THE RANKS

Li Yu (937 — 978)

For forty years,
    it's been my home and kingdom[1];
Extending three thousand *li's*[2],
    is the land my domain I call.

Phoenix pavilions and dragon towers
    rise to the sky;
Trees and flowers of jade hold me in thrall[3].

Do I ever know warfare at all?

Once taken prisoner[4],
My hair's turned grey, my waist small.

Hardest of all was the day of
    my fearful departure from the shrine,
While farewell songs
    were being played in the music hall.

Before the palace maids, I let my tears fall.

---

1 The kingdom of South Tang (南唐) was established in A.D. 937 by the poet's grandfather, Li Xing (李昇 A.D. 889-943) and was overthrown during the poet's reign in A.D. 975. The kingdom lasted for a period of 38 years.

2 One Chinese *li* equals about 0.3 mile.

破陣子

李煜 (937 — 978)

四十年來家國，三千里地山河。
鳳閣龍樓連霄漢，玉樹瓊枝作煙蘿。
幾曾識干戈？

一旦歸為臣虜，沉腰潘鬢消磨。
最是倉皇辭廟日，教坊猶奏別離歌。
垂淚對宮娥。

3 This is an allusion. He was held in the thrall of his own super-luxurious life in the palace like someone being entangled by vines in the hills.

4 Li Yu (the poet and the last king of South Tang) was taken prisoner upon surrender to the Song army in A.D. 975 and was poisoned to death by order of the Song Emperor (宋太宗) on the seventh day of the seventh month in A.D. 978.

ETERNAL LONGING

Li Yu (937 — 978)

Cloud-like tufted hair[1] is seen
Adorned with a jade hairpin.

Her dress is of flowing silk – pale and thin;
Her dark-green eyebrows slightly drawn in.

Endlessly whistles the autumn wind;
In unison, the pattering rain joins in.

Outside the blind,
   several plantain trees are making a din.
What a bleak, long night to be in!

1 Hair style popular with noble ladies in the late Tang Dynasty.

Background:
This lyric described an elegantly dressed lady being left alone in her boudoir longing for her love in a rainy night.

長相思

李煜 (937 — 978)

雲一緺，玉一梭，
澹澹衫兒薄薄羅，
　輕顰雙黛螺。

秋風多，雨相和，
簾外芭蕉三兩窠。
　夜長人奈何！

HEAVENLY BARBARIAN

Li Yu (937 — 978)

Dim is the moon shrouded in light mist
　　but flowers are bright –
What a good time to go to my love tonight!

In stockinged feet,
　　on the fragrant steps I land,
Gold-threaded shoes in my hand.

South of the painted hall he's in sight,
Trembling, momentarily I hold him tight.

"For me, stealing out is hard,
So, love me with all your heart!"

Background:
This lyric poem vividly described the secret meetings of the poet and the pretty younger sister of his queen, Queen Zhou (周后) around A.D. 964. Three years later, Queen Zhou passed away. The poet married the younger sister and made her the new queen in A.D. 967.

菩薩蠻

李煜 (937 — 978)

花明月黯籠輕霧，今宵好向郎邊去。
剗襪步香階，手提金縷鞋。

畫堂南畔見，一向偎人顫。
奴為出來難，教君恣意憐。

JADE TOWER SPRING

Li Yu (937 — 978)

In their new evening make-up
    with skin bright as snow,
Court ladies stream
    into the Spring Palace in a row.

The notes of Shengs[1] and flutes
    shoot into the sky;
All over the palace, again resounds
    the song of Skirts of Rainbow[2].

Who let perfumed chips in the wind blow?
Tapping the railing in drunkenness,
    my emotions overflow.

Light not red candles on the way home,
Clip-clopping on horse-back
    under a clear moon we'd go.

1 A traditional musical instrument consisting of a bundle of pipes of varying lengths attached
  to a bulb-shape holder.
2 The Skirts of Rainbow (霓裳羽衣曲), was the most popular court dancing music in Mid-
  Tang Dynasty.

玉樓春

李煜 (937 — 978)

晚妝初了明肌雪。
春殿嬪娥魚貫列。
笙簫吹斷水雲間，
重按霓裳歌遍徹。

臨風誰更飄香屑。
醉拍闌干情味切。
歸時休放燭花紅，
待踏馬蹄清夜月。

RIVER-TOWN

Reminisces of the Past in Jinling

Ouyang Jiong (869 — 971)

At day's end in Jinling[1],
    the grassy bank is calm;
Clouds turn rosy at sundown.

Heartless is the water –
It carries away the glories of the Six Dynasties[2]
Secretly amid its murmuring sound.

The moon above Gusu Terrace,
Like Xi Shi's[3] mirror,
    vainly shines on the river-town.

---

1 Today's Nanjing（南京）.

2 These were: Wu of the Three Kingdoms, East Jin, Song, Qi, Liang and Chen of the Southern dynasty,（三國吳、東晉、南朝宋、齊、梁、陳）. These dynasties all had their capital in Jinling and were all gone for one reason or another.

3 Xi Shi（西施）was a clothe-washing girl in the Kingdom of Yue which was conquered by Wu. King Yue（越王勾踐 B.C. 496-464）gave Xi Shi to King Wu（吳王夫差 B.C. 528-473）as part of a plot. Because of her matchless beauty, she became King Wu's beloved concubine with whom he spent all his energy and time. This resulted in the downfall of the Kingdom of Wu. King Yue eventually regained his kingdom.

江城子

金陵懷古

歐陽炯 (869 — 971)

晚日金陵岸草平，落霞明。
水無情。六代繁華，暗逐逝波聲。

空有姑蘇台上月，如西子鏡照江城。

RESENTMENT BY THE RIVER

Niu Qiao (850 — 920)

The east wind is fierce:
Repeatedly your hand I grip as parting nears.

Alone, I return to my chamber, heart-pierced.
Amid the patter of lingering rain on spring weeds,
the neigh of horses one hears[1].

Stand leaning by the door,
A word for my heartless lover:

"Scented powder mingles with tears."

---

1 The neigh of horses alluded to the departure of her lover in a carriage.

望江怨

牛嶠 (850 — 920)

東風急，惜別花時手頻執，
羅幃愁獨入。
馬嘶殘雨春蕪濕。

倚門立，寄語薄情郎：
粉香和淚泣。

HAWTHORNE

Niu Xiji (around 925)

The spring mountain mist was about to lift;
The sky was pale; stars sparse and small.

Cheeks lit by the fading moon:
At break of dawn,
      parting tears started to fall.

Much had been said:
Our love wasn't over at all.

Turning around, me you again told:

"Remember my green silk skirt,
And be compassionate
      to sweet grass wherever you go.[1]"

---

1 The speaker wore a green skirt. She told her lover to remember her wherever he came across
green grass.

生查子

牛希濟（約公元 925 年）

春山煙欲收，天澹稀星小。
殘月臉邊明，別淚臨清曉。

語已多，情未了，
回首猶重道：
記得綠羅裙，處處憐芳草。

DREAMING OF RIVER SOUTH

Huangfu Song (date of birth and death unknown)

The orchid-shape snuff¹ drops,
On the screen, dim turns the red plantain.

Leisurely I dream I'm in River South
 where plums are ripe,
And flutes being played
 in night boats in pattering rain.

By the bridge beside the courier post,
 voices of people reign.

1 The last portion of the candle or oil lamp wick which was burnt and charred forming a small
orchid-shape mass. The snuff would drop after the candle or lamp had completely burnt out
indicating that it was deep in the night.

Background:
The poet was recalling the days he spent in southern China.

夢江南

皇甫松（生卒年月不詳）

蘭燼落，屏上暗紅蕉。

閒夢江南梅熟日，夜船吹笛雨瀟瀟，
人語驛邊橋。

HEAVENLY BARBARIAN (1)

Wei Zhuang (836 — 910)

Sad was our parting in the red house[1] that night;
Half rolled-up was the fringed curtain
   in the perfumed lamp's light.

By the door under a fading moon in the skies,
Farewell you bade me with tear-filled eyes.

From your pi-pa adorned with feather and gold,
Melodies were like songs of an oriole.

You urged me to return early to your bower[2]:
By the green window, a beauty is like a flower[3].

1 Originally it meant the home of a rich family. Later it was used to mean the home of a lady.
2 Bedroom of a lady in the old days (閨房).
3 The poet hinted that a girl's beauty might not last long.

Background:
Wei Zhuang fled to River South during the Huang Chao Rebellion (黃巢之亂 A.D. 875-884). He wrote five Heavenly Divine lyric poems while he was living in Sichuan at old age reminiscing about the past. This first one recorded the poet's emotions during parting from his loved one.

菩薩蠻 (1)

韋莊 (836 — 910)

紅樓別夜堪惆悵，香燈半捲流蘇帳。
殘月出門時，美人和淚辭。

琵琶金翠羽，弦上黃鶯語。
勸我早歸家，綠窗人似花。

HEAVENLY BARBARIAN (2)

Wei Zhuang (836 — 910)

River South[1] is good, by everyone I was told:
It best befits travellers to stay here till old.

In spring, the water is bluer than the sky;
In a painted boat listening to the rain they lie.

The wine-shop maids are charming as the moon:
Their arms fair like frost and snow strewn.

Before getting old,
   a home trip one mustn't take:
Upon return one's heart will break.

1 South of the Yangtze River.

Background:
The second lyric poem recorded the poet's feelings as a traveller living amid beautiful sceneries and charming wine-shop maids in River South. He was, however, unable to return home because his home village was ravaged in a period of social chaos during the Huang Chao Rebellion (黃巢之亂 A.D. 875-884).

菩薩蠻 (2)

韋莊 (836 — 910)

人人盡說江南好，遊人只合江南老。
春水碧於天，畫船聽雨眠。

壚邊人似月，皓腕凝霜雪。
未老莫還鄉，還鄉須斷腸。

HEAVENLY BARBARIAN (3)

Wei Zhuang (836 — 910)

Now I recall the pleasurable times
    in River South that I had.
Youthful then,
    in light spring garments I was clad.

Riding on horseback,
    against the arched bridge I'd lean,
Red sleeves all over the house[1]
    would beckon me in.

Chains of gold fastened folding screens of jade;
Drunk, in the flower bush[2] the nights I stayed.

This time, if I should meet a spray[3],
I swear never to go home
    till my hair's turned grey.

1 Singsong house.
2 An allusion to the group of singsong girls inside the singsong house.
3 A spray of flowers. An allusion to a pretty girl.

Background:
The third lyric poem described the poet's carefree life as a young traveller in River South.

菩薩蠻 (3)

韋莊 (836 — 910)

如今卻憶江南樂，當時年少春衫薄。
騎馬倚斜橋，滿樓紅袖招。

翠屏金屈曲，醉入花叢宿。
此度見花枝，白頭誓不歸。

HEAVENLY BARBARIAN (4)

Wei Zhuang (836 — 910)

Let's get dead drunk tonight, my dear friend:
Talk not of matters
　　of tomorrow with wine in hand.

Cherish the host's kind-hearted reception;
Drink deep, for deep is our affection.

We'd worry spring nights are short;
When gold cups are full, complain not.

Let's guffaw before the wine:
How long after all is our lifetime!

Background:
The fourth lyric poem recorded an occasion during which the host urged the poet to drink himself drunk so as to ease the poet's sorrows for not being able to return to his home in Chang An (長安).

菩薩蠻 (4)

韋莊 (836 — 910)

勸君今夜須沉醉，樽前莫話明朝事。
　　珍重主人心，酒深情亦深。

　　須愁春漏短，莫訴金杯滿。
　　遇酒且呵呵，人生能幾何！

HEAVENLY BARBARIAN (5)

Wei Zhuang (836 — 910)

Beautiful is Luoyang City in springtime.
Away from home,
 a Luoyang scholar has past his prime.

Shady are the willows[1] on Prince Wei's mound,
Now I feel lost and down[2].

Peach blossoms by the spring water green,
Where bathing mandarin ducks[3] are seen.

With deep regret, I face the afterglow –
Oh, I miss you but you won't know.

---

1 It was believed that the phrase 'shady willows' was used to allude to the end of springtime because when summer replaced spring, willows grew thick and shady. It might also allude to the end of the Tang Dynasty.

2 At a time when the Tang Dynasty was toppled and Emperor Zhao Zong (昭宗) killed, the poet recalled his sad feelings amid the beautiful springtime in Luoyang.

3 Mandarin ducks live and fly in pairs, like lovebirds, which reminded him of his lover in Chang An.

Background:
In the fifth lyric poem, the poet recalled his times while he was in Luoyang and his sorrows for growing old away from home and for the demise of a dynasty. He felt sad that he might never be able to return to his loved one at home.

菩薩蠻 (5)

韋莊 (836 — 910)

洛陽城裏春光好，洛陽才子他鄉老。
柳暗魏王堤，此時心轉迷。

桃花春水綠，水上鴛鴦浴。
凝恨對殘輝，憶君君不知。

PURE SERENE MUSIC

Wei Zhuang (836 — 910)

The moon's fading as orioles cry;
The perfumed lamp
  in the ornate boudoir is put out thereby.

Outside the door,
  the horse neighs – his departure is nigh,
In a season when flowers say their last goodbye.

Make-up done but eyebrows left plain,
Against the golden door,
  she alone leans in pain.

Dust on the road mustn't be swept,
Or else longer away my love would remain[1].

1 An ancient custom especially among villagers.

清平樂

韋莊 (836 — 910)

鶯啼殘月，繡閣香燈滅。
門外馬嘶郎欲別，正是落花時節。

妝成不畫眉，含愁獨倚金扉。
去路香塵莫掃，掃即郎歸遲。

LOTUS LEAF CUP

Wei Zhuang (836 — 910)

I remember that year beneath the flowers,
At late hours.

When lady Xie[1] I first got to know,
The painted curtain
            at west of Water Hall hung low:
Holding hands, a will to meet again
            we did secretly show.

How regretful, under a fading moon
            at the dawn oriole's cry,
We said goodbye!

We've lost touch since then.
Now we're both in foreign domain,
There's no chance for us to meet again.

---

1 Name of a famous pretty singsong girl (Xie Qiuniang 謝秋娘) in Tang Dynasty. This term
was later used by poets to mean a pretty singsong girl.

荷葉盃

韋莊 (836 — 910)

記得那年花下，深夜。
初識謝娘時，
水堂西面畫簾垂，攜手暗相期。

惆悵曉鶯殘月，相別。
從此隔音塵。
如今俱是異鄉人，相見更無因。

A DISTANT HOME

Wei Zhuang (836 — 910)

Golden kingfisher,

Fly to the south for me –
     my message you'd deliver:

"A painted bridge the spring water nears….
Oh! Drunk I was under the flowers –
     for how many years?

Ever since we parted, full of shame I've been;
Teardrops I can't send over
     as we're far between.

Silk curtain, embroidered quilt and screen:
Bygone joys are but a dream."

歸國遙

韋莊 (836 — 910)

金翡翠，
為我南飛傳我意：
罨畫橋邊春水，幾年花下醉？

別後只知相愧，淚珠難遠寄。
羅幕鏽幃鴛被，舊歡如夢裏。

THE DAOIST PRIESTESS (1)

Wei Zhuang (836 — 910)

At midnight last night,
I dreamt about you all right.

A long talk we had –
Your face still pretty as peach blossoms,
Yet you kept lowering your head.

Unwilling to leave,
You were half shy but half glad.

I woke up and knew it was but a dream –
I was exceedingly sad.

女冠子 (1)

韋莊 (836 — 910)

昨夜夜半，
枕上分明夢見。

語多時。
依舊桃花面，頻低柳葉眉。

半羞還半喜，欲去又依依。
覺來知是夢，不勝悲。

THE DAOIST PRIESTESS (2)

Wei Zhuang (836 — 910)

The seventeenth of the fourth month is today:
It was last year on this very day.

Holding back my tears,
      I feigned hanging my head low
At the time of our parting.
Feeling shy, I half-knitted my eyebrows so.

I know not my heart's broken,
Only in dreams, with you I could go.

Except the moon on the sky's edge,
None would know.

女冠子 (2)

韋莊 (836 — 910)

四月十七，
正是去年今日。

別君時，
忍淚佯低面，含羞半斂眉。

不知魂已斷，空有夢相隨。
除卻天邊月，沒人知。

THREE TERRACES

Feng Yansi (903 — 960)

Bright moon! Bright moon!
You fill a lonely soul with extreme gloom.

Onto a mate-less bed
        at late hours, you beam:
No wonder it's a long night
        behind curtain and screen.

The night's long! The night's long!
To dream about the shady garden bower I long.

三臺令

馮延巳 (903 — 960)

明月！明月！
照得離人愁絕。

更深影入空牀，不
道幃屏夜長。

長夜！長夜！
夢到庭華陰下。

ETERNAL LONGING

Lin Bu (967 — 1028)

Mountains in Wu[1] are green;
Mountains in Yue[1] are also green.

Green mountains on riverbanks
    greet people[2] in between.
Who knows what emotions of parting mean?

With tears your eyes are dim;
With tears my eyes are also dim.

The chance of tying our love knots is slim.
Your boat's leaving
    now the tide has risen to the brim.

1 Small domain of feudal princes in the Zhou Dynasty by either side of the Qintong River
   around Zhejiang, Jiangsu and Anhui Provinces. Here the poet meant the mountains in the
   north and south.

2 People coming in and going out along the Qingtong River.

長相思

林逋 (967 — 1028)

吳山青，越山青，
兩岸青山相送迎。
　誰知離別情？

君淚盈，妾淚盈，
羅帶同心結未成。
　江頭潮已平。

HEAVENLY BARBARIAN

Lou Fu (Date of birth and death unknown)

Amid fine willow threads,
    orioles nearby sing;
Evening breezes caress
    the shadow of the swing.

Coming through the blind,
    I feel a sharp cold sting;
The lamp's burnt out but
    no dream my sleep can bring.

Into my ears your words flow:
"Wait for me by the flowers",
    with a smile, you point to show.

But you haven't returned even so,
All over the yard, flowers vainly blow.

菩薩蠻

樓扶（生卒年不詳）

絲絲楊柳鶯聲近，晚風吹過秋千影。
寒色一簾輕，燈殘夢不成。

耳邊消息在，笑指花梢待。
又是不歸來，滿庭花自開。

PHOENIX ON A WU-TUNG TREE

Liu Yong (987 — 1053)

I stand leaning in the lofty tower
    as gentle breezes blow.

Gazing at the far distance,
I see spring sorrows
    from the sky gloomily grow.

Amid the glitter of grass in the hazy afterglow,
Wordless by the rail,
    my sentiment who'd know?

Till drunk I'd recklessly indulge in my ale!

I drink and sing in pursuit of joy –
But to no avail.

My belt's becoming loose,
    still no regret would entail:
For her, it's worthwhile becoming drawn and pale.

蝶戀花

柳永 (987 — 1053)

佇倚危樓風細細。
望極春愁，黯黯生天際。
草色煙光殘照裏，無言誰會憑闌意？

擬把疏狂圖一醉。
對酒當歌，強樂還無味。
衣帶漸寬終不悔，為伊消得人憔悴。

BELLS IN THE RAIN

Liu Yong (987 — 1053)

Autumn cicadas mournfully sighed;
By the long pavilion,
The showers had just ceased at eventide.

Outside the city gate,
     we drank in a tent feeling depressed;
I lingered around,
But the magnolia boat's departure was nigh.

Grasping your hands,
     we stared at each other's tearful eyes –
Choked up and rendered speechless thereby.

I know after I've left, between us
Are thousands of miles of mist and waves –
Gloomy is the evening haze, vast the Chu[1] sky!

Since ancient times,
    passionate lovers part in dismay;
How could I bear this lonely, bleak autumn day!

Where would I be when I sober up tonight?
By a willowy bank,
In the morning breeze, the moon's fading away.

I'll be gone for years:
Wasted will be scenes beautiful and times gay.

However much tenderness I may feel,
To whom can I say?

1 The ancient Kingdom of Chu in the Warring States Period, B.C. 475-221 (春秋戰國時期
的楚國). It used to occupy a large area south of the Yangtze River. Here the word 'Chu'
was taken to mean 'southern'.

Background:
This is generally accepted as the most famous and touching farewell lyric poem written by Liu
Yong. In this legendary poem (possibly written in the magnolia boat), he recorded his extreme
grief and reluctance to leave his loved one during his departure from the capital for River South
to take up a new post.

雨霖鈴

柳永 (987 — 1053)

寒蟬淒切，
對長亭晚，驟雨初歇。

都門帳飲無緒，
留戀處，蘭舟催發。
執手相看淚眼，竟無語凝噎。

念去去，
千里煙波，暮靄沉沉楚天闊。

多情自古傷離別，
更那堪冷落清秋節！

今宵酒醒何處？
楊柳岸，曉風殘月。

此去經年，應是良辰好景虛設。
便縱有千種風情，更與何人說？

SANDS AT SILK-WASHING STREAM

Yan Shu (991 — 1055)

A new lyric for the tune and a cup of wine;
In the same old pavilion in last year's clime.

When will the setting sun
    again rise and shine?

Flowers fall and nothing can be done;
Swallows return like old acquaintances of mine.

Alone, I linger in a fragrant path
    in the small garden taking my time.

Background:

Yan Shu was a prodigy, statesman and well-known poet. He was conferred the title of Jinshi (進士) by Emperor Song Zhenzong (宋真宗) at the age of 14. He joined the civil service and became the Prime Minister (宰相) in A.D. 1042.

浣溪沙

晏殊 (991 — 1055)

一曲新詞酒一杯，
去年天氣舊亭臺，
夕陽西下幾時迴？

無可奈何花落去，
似曾相識燕歸來，
小園香徑獨徘徊。

JADE TOWER SPRING

Yan Shu (991 — 1055)

After the swallows and wild geese,
    orioles are homeward-bound.
In this floating life, I'd carefully count
    the myriad things that came around.

How much longer than spring dreams
    did they stay?
They scattered like autumn clouds
    and nowhere to be found.

A tune from the lute[1]; the girdle-gem
    an immortal lover unbound[2]....
But she won't stay
    however hard I held on to her silken gown.

I'd urge you, my dear friend,
    never alone be the sober one:
Get dead drunk among the flowers –
    chances to do so in life never abound.

1 Based on the love story wherein Zhuo Wenjun (卓文君), a widow, was seduced by a tune from the lute played by Sima Xiangru (司馬相如). She ran away with Sima on the same night.

2 Based on the story wherein Zheng Jiaofu (鄭交甫) befriended two pretty girls by the riverbank. The girls unbound their girdle gems and gave them to Zheng as souvenirs and left. After a short walk, Zheng was saddened to find that the gems were gone, so were the girls. It was believed the girls were fairies.

玉樓春

晏殊 (991 — 1055)

燕鴻過後鶯歸去，細算浮生千萬緒。
長於春夢幾多時，散似秋雲無覓處。

聞琴解珮神仙侶，挽斷羅衣留不住。
勸君莫作獨醒人，爛醉花間應有數。

TREADING THE SEDGE

Yan Shu (991 — 1055)

On the small path, reds[1] are scarce;
In the fragrant countryside,
    all is covered with green[2].

In the dark shade of trees,
    lofty towers are vaguely seen.

The spring wind knows not
    how to restrain willow flowers –
Like drizzles, they randomly
    caress passer-by's cheeks and chin.

Orioles hide behind emerald leaves;
Swallows are kept out by the vermilion screen.

Incense from the burner tranquilly coils
    around drifting gossamer therein.

The setting sun again
    shines on the deep, deep courtyard
As I wake up from a melancholy, drunken dream.

1 Red flowers.
2 Green trees and grass.

踏莎行

晏殊 (991 — 1055)

小徑紅稀，芳郊綠遍，
　高臺樹色陰陰見。
春風不解禁楊花，濛濛亂撲行人面。

翠葉藏鶯，朱簾隔燕，
　鑪香靜逐游絲轉。
一場愁夢酒醒時，斜陽卻照深深院。

PURE SERENE MUSIC

Yan Shu (991 — 1055)

On red paper in characters fine,
She lays bare her mind.

The wild goose[1] is in the clouds,
      the fish[1] in the brine;
How depressing, a messenger she can't find.

At sunset in the western tower, alone she'd lean;
The distant hill happens to
      face the hook of the window screen.

Her loved one is nowhere to be found…
Eastward the water continues to flow and as green.

---

1 In the old days, people in despair sometimes hoped the wild goose or the fish would carry
  their messages to their loved ones as communication was extremely difficult. These two
  words 'goose and fish' later meant communication in the Chinese language (魚雁相通).

清平樂

晏殊 (991 — 1055)

紅牋小字，説盡平生意。
鴻雁在雲魚在水，惆悵此情難寄。

斜陽獨倚西樓，遙山恰對簾鈎。
人面不知何處，綠波依舊東流。

HAWTHORN

Ouyang Xiu (1007 — 1072)

Last year on Lantern Festival[1] night,
Lanterns in the flower fair bright as daylight.

The moon rose above the willows:
We dated in the twilight.

This year on Lantern Festival night,
The moon and lanterns remain bright.

My love of last year is nowhere to be found:
Tears wetted my spring sleeves outright.

---

1 Lantern Festival is also known as the Chinese lovers' day. It falls on the fifteenth day of the
first month in the lunar calendar, i.e. the first full moon in the new year.

生查子

歐陽修 (1007 — 1072)

去年元夜時，花市燈如畫。
月上柳梢頭，人約黃昏後。

今年元夜時，月與燈依舊，
不見去年人，淚濕春衫袖。

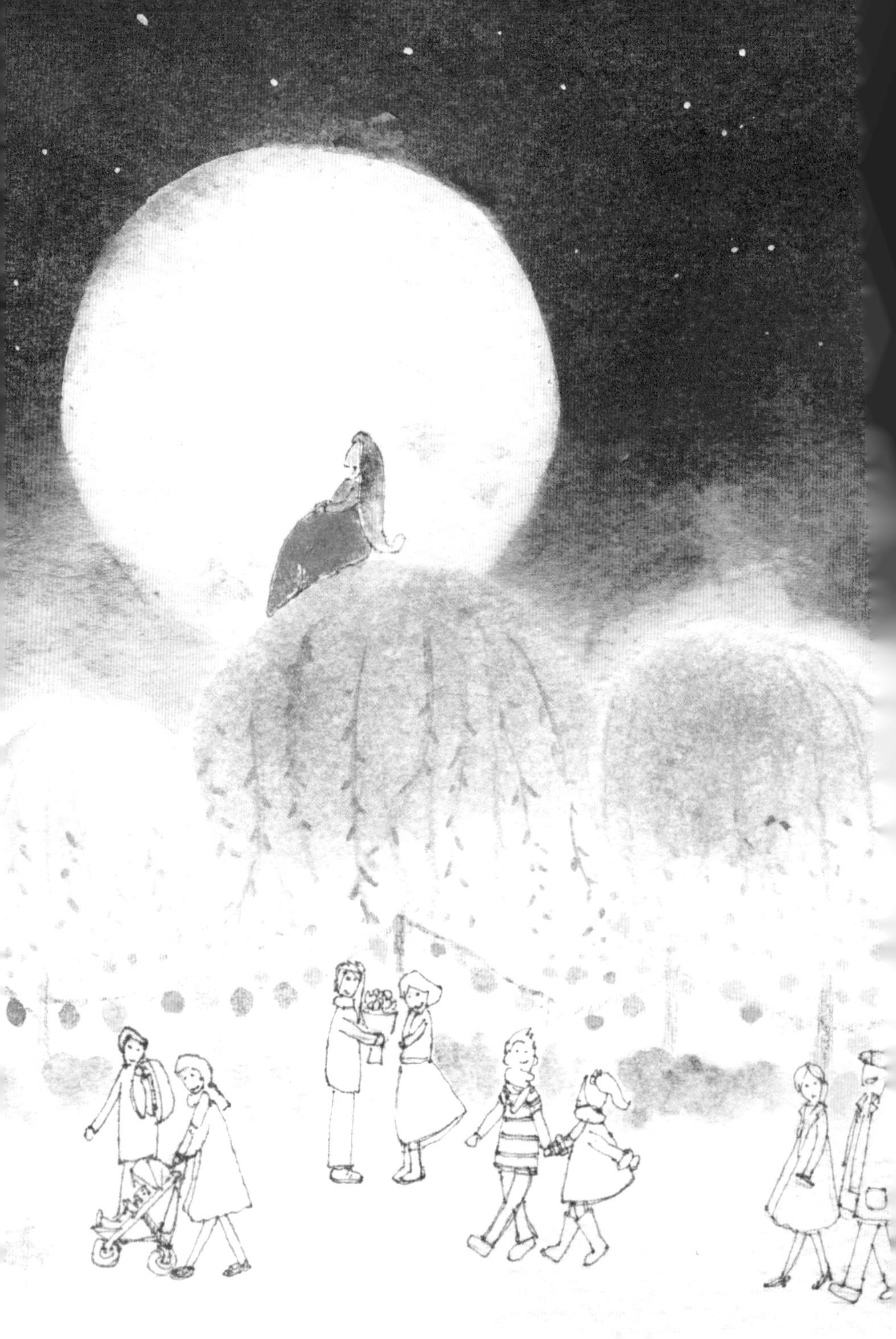

JADE TOWER SPRING (1)

Ouyang Xiu (1007 — 1072)

Before the wine,
    I meant to announce my departure date.
Hardly had I begun when
    you choked back tears in a miserable state.

In life, how crazy one is when in love;
To this regret neither the wind
    nor the moon would relate.

A new parting song we mustn't create:
One is enough to twist my bowels into a plait[1].

Only after flowers in Luoyang[2] are all seen,
Would I find it easy to part from my mate[3].

---

1 An allusion to a person being placed in an extremely sorrowful condition.

2 Luoyang is a city in northern China in the Henan Province which is famous for its flowers. Its nickname is Flower City. Flowers are so plentiful in the city that it is nearly impossible to see all the flowers. He was unwilling to leave Luoyang.

3 In the original text, the poet used 'spring wind' to allude to his beloved mate. Spring wind was considered gentle and very lovely in those days.

玉樓春 (1)

歐陽修 (1007 — 1072)

尊前擬把歸期說，未語春容先慘咽。
人生自是有情癡，此恨無關風與月。

離歌且莫翻新闋，一曲能教腸寸結。
直須看盡洛城花，始共春風容易別。

Background:
The poet was an official posted in Luoyang in the year 1031, aged 24. He was due to return to the capital, Chang An at the expiry of his posting in 1034. He wrote this poem at a farewell banquet in the presence of his lover.

JADE TOWER SPRING (2)

Ouyang Xiu (1007 — 1072)

This time in Luoyang,
   trees are flowering everywhere.
Blossoms are gorgeous,
   sweet scent now and then fills the air.

Drifting gossamer
   deliberately entangles us tight.
For no reason, weeping willows
   vie to bid farewell to a parting pair.

In the green mountain pass,
   red apricot blossoms flare.
Downhill, travellers seek lodging and care.

Tonight, who'd keep me company from afar?
None but the moon
   above the silent, lonely inn over there.

Background:
The poet recorded his feelings when he left Luoyang in a blossoming spring in A.D. 1034. He said goodbye to his loved one under willow trees and was eventually left alone sleepless inside a silent, lonely inn.

玉樓春 (2)

歐陽修 (1007 — 1072)

洛陽正值芳菲節，穠艷清香相間發。
遊絲有意苦相縈，垂柳無端爭贈別。

杏花紅處青山缺，山畔行人山下歇。
今宵誰肯遠相隨？惟有寂寥孤館月。

JADE TOWER SPRING (3)

Ouyang Xiu (1007 — 1072)

After you left,
  I know not if you're near or faraway.
All looks dreary – oh, how grey!

As you travel farther and farther,
  gradually no letter comes.
Where can I ask now that
  the river is wide, the fish[1] gone astray?

Deep in the night,
  an autumn tune the wind and bamboos play:
Myriad leaves lament in a thousand voices –
  regrets they all convey.

So, I look for you in dreams on my lone pillow,
No dreams come –
  besides, the lamp's burning out anyway.

---

1 Fish and wild geese were symbols for messengers in the old days.

Background:
This poem described a woman at home pining for her loved one who had gone on a faraway journey.

玉樓春 (3)

歐陽修 (1007 — 1072)

別後不知君遠近，觸目淒涼多少悶！
漸行漸遠漸無書，水闊魚沈何處問？

夜深風竹敲秋韻，萬葉千聲皆是恨。
故欹單枕夢中尋，夢又不成燈又燼。

ETERNAL LONGING (1)

Ouyang Xiu (1007 — 1072)

Flowers are like you,
Willows are like you.

Flowers and willows were young[1]
    when we bade each other adieu.
Bowing your head, tears you burst into.

East of the Yangtze River,
West of it too.

On both shores,
    separately mandarin ducks[2] flew.
As to when they'll meet again none has a clue.

---

1 An allusion. The poet in fact meant they were young when they parted.

2 Like love birds, mandarin ducks normally live and fly in pairs but he saw them flying in separate directions. Again, the poet alluded to the situation of himself and his lover.

長相思 (1)

歐陽修 (1007 — 1072)

花似伊，柳似伊，
花柳青春人別離。
低頭雙淚垂。

長江東，長江西，
兩岸鴛鴦兩處飛。
相逢知幾時。

ETERNAL LONGING (2)

Ouyang Xiu (1007 — 1072)

All over the stream, duckweeds lie;
Around the bank, willows wind.

West of the stream I bade him goodbye.
When I returned, the moon
    hung low over the hills in the sky.

Thick mist drifts by;
Bleak winds sigh.

Leaning by the scarlet door again,
    I hear his horse cry.
In the bitter cold, separately gulls fly.

Background:
This lyric described a woman who had parted from her lover in a misty, windy and bitterly cold morning. She returned home alone and leant against the door. She seemed to hear the sound of his horse and was sad to see gulls flying by separately.

長相思 (2)

歐陽修 (1007 — 1072)

蘋滿溪，柳繞堤，
相送行人溪水西。
回時隴月低。

煙霏霏，風淒淒，
重倚朱門聽馬嘶。
寒鷗相對飛。

WAVES WASHING SANDS

Ouyang Xiu (1007 — 1072)

Wine in hand, the east wind¹ I ask
Not to go away so fast.

Weeping willows and purple paths in
    Luoyang east we visited in the past.
Hand in hand, we toured flower bushes,
Missing not a single mass.

How bitter, our separation comes so fast!
This regret will never pass.

Flowers this year are prettier than last.
What a pity, flowers may be prettier next year,
But who'll share them with us?

1 East wind (also called spring wind) blows in springtime in Luoyang City. Here the poet was
alluding to springtime. He prayed that springtime could stay longer.

Background:
At the time when the poet was a court official posted in Luoyang City in A.D. 1031, he had a
happy tour in the east of the city in springtime with three other officials and they thoroughly
enjoyed admiring flowers and reciting poems. In the following year, he felt a bit down as some
of his colleagues were transferred or about to be transferred to other posts.

浪淘沙

歐陽修 (1007 — 1072)

把酒祝東風，且共從容。
垂楊紫陌洛城東。
總是當年攜手處，遊遍芳叢。

聚散苦匆匆，此恨無窮。
今年花勝去年紅。
可惜明年花更好，知與誰同？

PICKING MULBERRY LEAVES (1)

Ouyang Xiu (1007 — 1072)

The West Lake's lovely
    after the blossoms are gone:
Only untidy heaps of faded reds remain.

Catkins fly like drizzling rain;
By the railing under the sweeping willows,
    all day long the winds reign.

When music and songs have ceased
    and revellers left,
One's feeling for spring is but vain.

I lower the blind over the window pane:
A pair of swallows[1] returns in the gentle rain.

---

1 The poet used a pair of swallows to contrast his loneliness.

採桑子 (1)

歐陽修 (1007 — 1072)

羣芳過後西湖好，浪籍殘紅。
飛絮濛濛，
垂柳闌干盡日風。

笙歌散盡遊人去，始覺春空。
垂下簾攏，
雙燕歸來細雨中。

PICKING MULBERRY LEAVES (2)

Ouyang Xiu (1007 — 1072)

I love the beautiful West Lake all my life.
When I first came, a scarlet carriage¹ I rode.

Like floating clouds,
        riches and honour come and go.
Twenty springs have since passed before I know.

Coming back to this place,
        I'm like the crane of Liao Dong².
The city and its people –
What a difference they now show.

Who'd recognise their master of long ago?

1 A carriage used exclusively for high-ranking officials in those days.

2 The ancient legend has it that a man in Liao Dong once left home to study Daoism in the
   mountains and became immortal. He subsequently changed into a crane and returned
   home after a thousand years. He found his home city and its people had all changed beyond
   recognition. An archer even tried to shoot him. He flew away and never returned.

採桑子 (2)

歐陽修 (1007 — 1072)

平生為愛西湖好，來擁朱輪，
富貴浮雲，
俯仰流年二十春。

歸來恰似遼東鶴，城郭人民，
觸目皆新，
誰識當年舊主人？

Background:
The poet was appointed as the magistrate of Yingzhou (潁 州) in A.D. 1049. He retired in A.D. 1071. He returned to Yingzhou (潁州) after over 20 years of imperial service in various places.

BUTTERFLIES IN LOVE WITH FLOWERS

Ouyang Xiu (1007 — 1072)

Deep, deep lies the courtyard –
    how deep does one know?

Thick, thick are the willows –
    like a bank of mist;
Countless screens and curtains one'd behold.

Horses with jade bridles and carved saddles[1] –
    to singsong houses[2] how often they go!
Tall houses block my view of Zhang Tai Row[3].

Amid slashing rain and blustering wind,
    the third month waves goodbye. [4]

Doors are shut at dusk,

But to make spring stay fail I.

I ask the flowers with teary eye…
They speak not –
    over the swing, scattered red petals fly.

1 This is an allusion. It indirectly refers to rich people frequenting singsong houses in luxurious carriages drawn by noble horses.

2 A euphemism for brothels, sometimes called 'blue chambers' (青樓).

3 Originally it was the name of a street in the city of Chang An (today's Xian 長安市即今日之西安) in Han Dynasty. It was later known as a place where singsong girls lived after a story written about a famous singsong girl called Liu (即章台柳) living in this area.

4 When the third month came to an end, spring had already gone. The third month on the lunar calendar is roughly equivalent to April.

蝶戀花

歐陽修 (1007 — 1072)

庭院深深深幾許？
楊柳堆煙，簾幕無重數。
玉勒雕鞍遊冶處，樓高不見章台路。

雨橫風狂三月暮。
門掩黃昏，無計留春住。
淚眼問花花不語，亂紅飛過鞦韆去。

Background:
This lyric poem describes the plight of a lady being left alone inside a large mansion with large, deep courtyards and gardens. Isolated by countless curtains and screens, she felt lonesome and empty in late spring. Her loved one, probably her rich husband, stayed out most of the times paying visits to singsong houses. She was also saddened to see her youth vainly passed away, as spring (i.e. the third month) was ending and flowers were falling.

WATERBAG DANCE
Sorrows of Separation

Fan Zhongyan (989 — 1052)

Yellow leaves carpet the ground;
Bluish clouds embellish the skies.

Autumn hues tint the waves
Where chilly and emerald mists rise.

The hills glow in the slanting sun
Where the water meets the skies.

The fragrant grass is heartless –
Outside the slanting sun, it lies.

A gloomy soul pining for home,
I recall a traveller's plight.

Except when a sweet dream comes,
I sleep not, night after night.

Never lean alone in a tower
in the bright moonlight.

Wine, once inside sorrowful bowels,
Turns into homesick tears outright.

Background:
This poem was written in the autumn of A.D. 1040 in Yanzhou (延 州) in today's YanAn (延 安) in Shaanxi Province. The poet was the General in command of an army stationed there fighting against the invading barbarians outside the Great Wall. He was homesick in the desolate wilderness of the frontier.

蘇幕遮

別恨

范仲淹 (989 — 1052)

碧雲天，黃葉地。
秋色連波，波上寒煙翠。

山映斜陽天接水。
芳草無情，更在斜陽外。

黯鄉魂，追旅思。
夜夜除非，好夢留人睡。

明月高樓休獨倚。
酒入愁腸，化作相思淚。

PARTRIDGE WEATHER (1)

Yan Jidao (1030 — 1106)

Cordially serving wine in jade cups,
    colourful sleeves you were in.
In those days, I feared not to drink
    till I flushed my cheeks and chin.

You danced till the moon over the tower
    sank below the willows;
You sang till the peach blossom fan
    exhausted its wind.

Since we parted,

Thoughts of our encounter gleam.

How many times I met you in my dream?

Tonight, I must shine on you
    with this silver lamp,
For fear our reunion now is but a dream.

Background:

The poet was the son of Yan Shu (晏 殊), the Prime Minister who was also a well-known poet. This poem was written to record the poet's deep emotions upon re-uniting with his love after a prolonged separation. He could not believe it was real as he described it in the last two lines.

鷓鴣天 (1)

晏幾道 (1030 — 1106)

彩袖殷勤捧玉鍾，當年拚卻醉顏紅。
舞低楊柳樓心月，歌盡桃花扇底風。

從別後，憶相逢。幾回魂夢與君同？
今宵剩把銀釭照，猶恐相逢在夢中。

PARTRIDGE WEATHER (2)

Yan Jidao (1030 — 1106)

Amid a short lyric before the wine,
    Yuxiao[1] I set my eyes upon.
By the silver lamps,
    too bewitching was she and her song.

Drunk I fell during the song –
    who could I blame?
Home I went after the party –
    the tipsiness hadn't gone.

Springtime's quiet;
The night goes on and on …
The way to the azure sky and Chu Palace is long[2].

In my dream, I've the habit of
    ignoring restraints,
Treading on willow flowers,
    again the Xie's Bridge[3] I walked along.

---

1 Name of a legendary beautiful singing girl before the poet's time. The poet used this name here to mean a beautiful singing girl.

2 The poet was bewitched by this girl but he knew because of his high social position, they were therefore very far apart. He could only pay her visits in his dream. Chu Palace here alluded to the place where Yuxiao lived.

3 The place where a famous singing girl named Xie Qiuniang (謝秋娘) once lived. This term was later used by poets to mean the home of a singing girl.

鷓鴣天 (2)

晏幾道 (1030 — 1106)

小令尊前見玉簫，銀燈一曲太妖嬈。
歌中醉倒誰能恨？唱罷歸來酒未消。

春悄悄，夜迢迢，碧雲天共楚宮遙。
夢魂慣得無拘檢，又踏楊花過謝橋。

BUTTERFLIES IN LOVE WITH FLOWERS

Yan Jidao (1030 — 1106)

Drunk, I left the West Tower[1] –
    sobered up, I wish I could forget[2].

Like spring dreams and autumn clouds[3],
Parting came so easily after we met.

By the window half-full of
    slanting moonlight, little sleep did I get;
On the painted screen,
    the verdant hills of Wu[4] are casually set.

Wine stains on my coat and
    words in poems we read;

In dots and in lines,
Sadness they all spread.

Unable to help,
    the red candle pities itself instead:
In the cold night, for me tears[5] it vainly shed.

---

1 A common name in ancient times for a place where banquets for officials and scholars were held. Music and singsong girls were often provided. The poet had some memorable times in such a place.

2 Although reluctant to recall, the poet was, in fact, unable to forget his romantic encounter in the West Tower.

蝶戀花

晏幾道 (1030 — 1106)

醉別西樓醒不記。

春夢秋雲，聚散真容易。

斜月半窗還少睡。畫屏閒展吳山翠。

衣上酒痕詩裏字。

點點行行，總是淒涼意。

紅燭自憐無好計。夜寒空替人垂淚。

3 A traditional Chinese metaphor meaning from nowhere something comes and into nowhere it disappears, just like dreams and clouds that are unpredictable and uncontrollable.

4 The area around the former Kingdom of Wu in the Zhou Dynasty by the north side of the Qiantang River around Zhejiang, Jiangsu and Anhui Provinces. Here the poet meant the mountains in the north.

5 Wax drops that fell from a burning candle were likened to tears people shed.

PRELUDE TO WATER MUSIC

Su Shi (1037 — 1101)

**At Mid-Autumn Festival in the year Bing Chen
(1076), I drank to my heart's content till dawn
and became very drunk. I wrote this poem,
also thinking of Ziyou.**

When did the bright moon come into being?
Holding my wine, I ask the dark sky.

I know not what year it is tonight
In the celestial palace on high.

I wish to fly back with the wind's aid,
Yet fear that marble towers and halls of jade,
Are so high up that unbearable cold I'd find.

I rise to dance and
      frolic with my lonely shadow –
How can it compare to life among mankind?

Around the scarlet pavilion,
Through the carved window,
On the sleepless the moon shines.

A grudge there shouldn't be,
But then why is she always full
      during people's parting times?

Men have their joy and sorrow,
　　　their parting and meeting;
The moon has her dim and bright times,
　　　her waxing and waning.

Since ancient times, nothing's perfect anyway.

I only wish we'd both live long,
To share the moon's splendour,
　　　a thousand miles away.

Background:
This legendary lyric poem was written on Mid-Autumn Festival night in A.D. 1076 when Su Shi was serving as the magistrate in Mizhou (密州) in today's Zhu City, Shandong Province. Traditionally, this was a time for reunion with family and friends in China. He missed his younger brother Su Zhe (蘇轍), nickname Zi You (子由) who served in the Governor's Office in Qizhou (齊州) in today's Jinan, also in Shandong Province. The two brothers had not met for seven years.

水調歌頭

蘇軾 (1037 — 1101)

丙辰中秋，歡飲達旦，大醉，作此篇，兼懷子由。

明月幾時有？把酒問青天。
不知天上宮闕，今夕是何年？

我欲乘風歸去，惟恐瓊樓玉宇，
高處不勝寒。
起舞弄清影，何似在人間？

轉朱閣，低綺戶，照無眠。
不應有恨，何事長向別時圓？

人有悲歡離合，月有陰晴圓缺，
此事古難全。
但願人長久，千里共嬋娟。

THE CHARM OF NIANNU

Thinking of the ancient time at the Red Cliff

Su Shi (1037 — 1101)

Eastward rolls the Great River[1].

Its waves have washed away

Brilliant men of a thousand ages along its flow.

West of the old rampart,

Lies the red cliff[2] of Master Zhou[3]
> of the Three Kingdoms – they say so.

Jumbled rocks pierce the sky;

Raging waves batter against the bank,

Whirling up a thousand mounds of snow.

Beautiful as a picture
> are the River and the hills –

It was a time of many a hero!

I can visualize Gongjin[4] in those days,

Having just married the younger Qiao[5],

Gallant and with a demeanour truly divine.

1 The Yangtze River.

2 Located along the Yangtze River in today's Red Cliff County, Hebei Province, the Red Cliff was the site of a famous battle in A.D. 208 in the East Han Dynasty (A.D. 25-220).

3 & 4 Zhou Yu (周瑜) (A.D. 175-210), commander of the allied forces of Wu (吳國) and Shu (蜀國) who, with only 50,000 warriors, crushed the much stronger enemy troops in a battle along the Yangtze River in the Three Kingdoms Period (A.D. 220-280).

5 The two beautiful sisters are known as big Qiao and small Qiao (大喬及小喬). The elder sister married Sun Ce (孫策 - 孫權之兄).

Feathered fan in hand, silk turban on his head,

While chatting and laughing,

He reduced the enemy fleet to
    flying ashes and smoke on the battle line[6].

To this old country their spirits would roam[7]....

They'd laugh at me for being sentimental,

And at the premature white hair of mine.

Life's like a dream:

Let me pour offering to
    the moon in the River with this wine.

6 Zhou torched the entire fleet of Cao Cao (曹操) on the battle line and won complete victory. Cao Cao (曹操) (A.D. 155-220), the Prime Minister of East Han (東漢), led a huge fleet with 200,000 warriors on numerous big battleships down the Yangtze River to invade the south.

7 The poet imagined the spirits of heroes of the Three Kingdoms were roaming in Red Cliff and laughing at him while he was writing the poem.

Background:

This is the most popular lyric poem of Su Shi. It was written in A.D. 1082. It is well-known for the powerful and vivid description of the Yangtze River, the red cliff and how the large fleet of Cao Cao (曹操) was torched by Zhou Yu (周瑜) in the historic Battle of the Red Cliff.

念奴嬌

赤壁懷古

蘇軾 (1037 — 1101)

大江東去，
浪淘盡，千古風流人物。

故壘西邊，
人道是：三國周郎赤壁。

亂石穿空，
驚濤拍岸，捲起千堆雪。
江山如畫，一時多少豪傑。

遙想公瑾當年，
小喬初嫁了，雄姿英發。

羽扇綸巾，
談笑間，檣櫓灰飛煙滅。

故國神遊，
多情應笑我，早生華髮。
人生如夢，一尊還酹江月。

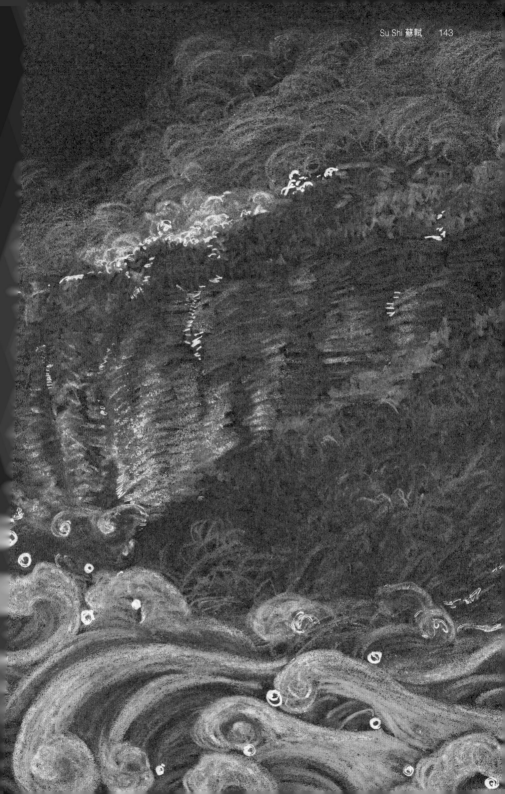

THE RIVER TOWN

(Recording my dream on the 20th night of the first month in the year 1075)

Su Shi (1037 — 1101)

For ten years, the living and the dead
    are lost in despair.

To think of you I can't bear,
But to forget you I can ne'er.

A thousand miles away
    you're in a solitary grave:
My grief there's no one to share.

You won't recognize me even if we met –
Weather-beaten is my face,
Frosty my temple hair.

Last night, in a gloomy dream,
    I was suddenly home.

By the window in the small room,
You were arranging your hair with a comb.

At each other we stared, speechless…
Only a thousand lines of tears were shown.

I know year after year on moonlit nights,
At the Short Pine Mound[1],
Heartbroken I'm prone.

---

1 The place where the poet's wife was buried in Sichuan Province.

江城子

乙卯正月廿日記夢

蘇軾 (1037 — 1101)

十年生死兩茫茫。
不思量，自難忘。

千里孤墳，無處話淒涼。
縱使相逢應不識，塵滿面，鬢如霜。

夜來幽夢忽還鄉。
小軒窗，正梳妝。

相顧無言，惟有淚千行。
料得年年腸斷處，明月夜，短松崗。

Background:
The poet recorded his dream in this poem ten years after the death of his wife in the year
1065. He was serving in Mizhou (密州) and missed her very much.

THE DIVINER

Written during my stay in Dinghui Lodge in Huangzhou

Su Shi (1037 — 1101)

A waning moon hangs over
    a gaunt Wutong tree,
The water-clock stops dripping –
    all becomes quiet outright[1].

Who sees the exile[2] pacing to and fro alone?
A lone wild goose whose dim shadow's in sight.

Startled, it throws its head back –
No one understands its plight.

It picks over cold branches but roosts on none:
Yet lands on the shoal, lonely and bleak despite.

---

1 The water-clock stopped dripping when water inside it ran out indicating that it was deep in the night.

2 The poet himself. See 'Background' below.

卜算子

黃州定慧院寓居所作

蘇軾 (1037 — 1101)

缺月掛疏桐，漏斷人初靜。
誰見幽人獨往來？
縹緲孤鴻影。

驚起卻回頭，有恨無人省。
揀盡寒枝不肯棲，
寂寞沙洲冷。

Background:
As an offender of the Court for his involvement in the Wu Tai Poems Case (烏臺詩案) the poet was banished. He lived in exile in Huangzhou (黃州) in today's Huang Gang in Hubei Province in A.D. 1080. This poem alluded to the situation of the poet after his narrow escape. He likened himself to a lone frightened wild goose which chose to roost on a lonely and bleak shoal instead of roosting on a branch high up on a tree (i.e. in a high position).

YOUTHFUL PLEASURE

Su Shi (1037 — 1101)

Last year, I saw you off
Outside the Yu Hang[1] city gate:
Like willow flowers was the fluttering snow.

This year, spring has ended:
Like snow are the willow flowers,
But you haven't returned home even so.

I roll up the curtain
      to invite the moon to my wine,
Through the window gauze
      comes the dew as the winds blow.

It's like the moon's having pity
      on a pair of perching swallows[2] –
On the painted beam,
It casts its slanting glow.

---

1 One of the three city gates in northern Hangzhou (杭州) in Song Dynasty.

2 A pair of perching swallows deepened the poet's lonesome feelings while longing for the
  return of his mate.

少年遊

蘇軾 (1037 — 1101)

去年相送，餘杭門外，
　飛雪似楊花。

今年春盡，楊花似雪，
　猶不見還家。

對酒捲簾邀明月，
　風露透窗紗。

恰似姮娥憐雙燕，分明照，
　畫樑斜。

THE DIVINER

Li Zhiyi (1035 — 1117)

I live at the upper end and
You live at the lower end of the Yangtze River.

Every day, I pine for you but see you not….
Though we both drink from the same river!

When will this river cease to flow?
When will this regret come to an end?

I only wish your heart would be like mine:
My longing for you would prove not misspent.

卜算子

李之儀 (1035 — 1117)

我住長江頭，君住長江尾。
日日思君不見君，共飲長江水。

此水幾時休？此恨何時已？
只願君心似我心，定不負相思意。

IMMORTALS AT MAGPIE BRIDGE

Qin Guan (1049 — 1100)

Delicately, fine ribbons of clouds intertwine;
Stars shoot across the night sky
 transmitting regret…

Secretly, the Cowherd and the Weaver Girl[1]
 cross the far off Milky Way.

Amid golden[2] wind and
 jade-like dews they meet.
They're happier than the
 countless separated lovers[3] on earth anyway.

Tender as water is their love;
Sweet as a dream their reunion,

But how unbearable to see, on the Magpie Bridge[4],
 each other's homeward way!

---

1 Two stars positioned on either side of the Milky Way. Chinese legend has it that they are
 heavenly lovers. The couple can meet only once a year on the night of the seventh day of the
 seventh lunar month when countless magpies would form a bridge to enable them to cross
 the Milky Way. This day is also known as Chinese Valentine's Day.

2 During autumn in northern China, leaves and crops change into golden colour. Hence,
 autumn wind is also called golden wind.

3 The poet used the allusion made by Li Ying's 'Poem on the seventh night of the seventh
 month' (李郢七夕詩 : 莫嫌天上稀相見，猶勝人間去不回) which lamented the
 endless separations of lovers on earth while the heavenly lovers could at least enjoy their
 yearly reunion on this night.

4 A bridge formed by countless magpies in the sky according to the legend.

If love is meant to be truly eternal,
It shouldn't hinge on
      meeting each other day after day.

鵲橋仙

秦觀 (1049 — 1100)

纖雲弄巧，飛星傳恨，
銀漢迢迢暗渡。
金風玉露一相逢，便勝卻人間無數。

柔情似水，佳期如夢，
忍顧鵲橋歸路。
兩情若是長久時，又豈在朝朝暮暮。

AS IN A DREAM

Qin Guan (1049 — 1100)

Like water, the night's long and deep.
Fiercely blowing is the wind –
    tightly shut the courier post[1] they keep.

My dream's interrupted
    when at the lamp mice peep[2],
The frost's bringing in the morning chill –
    into my quilt it'd creep.

Can't sleep!
Can't sleep!

Outside the door, horses neigh –
    into action people leap[3].

---

1 Courier posts were used as hostels primarily for travelling officials in ancient times.

2 Hungry mice in the middle of the night peeped at the lamp wanting to drink the oil inside.

3 Servants got up at daybreak to prepare for another day's journey outside the door.

如夢令

秦觀 (1049 — 1100)

遙夜沉沉如水。
風緊驛亭深閉。
夢破鼠窺燈，霜送曉寒侵被。

無寐！
無寐！
門外馬嘶人起。

Background:
The poet was a court official travelling to take up a new post in A.D. 1096. He spent the night in a courier post and was awakened in the middle of the night by the howling wind and the squeaks of mice. The morning chill kept him from sleeping till dawn.

PURE SERENE MUSIC

Huang Tingjian (1045 — 1105)

Spring has gone – where's she?
In this lonely place, no traces of her can one see.

Should anyone know where spring may be,
Call her back to live with me.

Spring left no footprints –
        her whereabouts who knows?
Unless we ask the golden orioles.

But no one understands
        their incessant trill,
And they fly past the roses as the wind blows.

清平樂

黃庭堅 (1045 — 1105)

春歸何處？
寂寞無行路。
若有人知春去處，喚取歸來同住。

春無蹤跡誰知？
除非問取黃鸝。
百囀無人能解，因風飛過薔薇。

HALF-DEAD WUTUNG

He Zhu (1052 — 1125)

All has changed
    when Chang Men[1] again I passed by.
We came here together
    but not returning together – why?

The Wutong's half-dead[2]
    after the autumn frost;
A white-haired lovebird's left to solitarily fly.

Dews on the grass in the meadow begin to dry[3],
I linger around our old home
    and the new grave where you lie.

In an empty bed by the south window,
    I listen to the rain …
Who'd mend my clothes
    at night under the lamp by and by?

---

1 West Gate in Suzhou City.

2 This is a metaphor. A half-dead Wutong tree stands for someone who has lost his/her spouse.

3 The poet hinted that life was short like dews on the grass.

半死桐

賀鑄 (1052 — 1125)

重過閶門萬事非。同來何事不同歸？
梧桐半死清霜後，頭白鴛鴦失伴飛。

原上草，露初晞，舊棲新壟兩依依。
空牀臥聽南窗雨，誰復挑燈夜補衣？

Background:
The poet wrote his poem to commemorate his wife after he returned to his old home in Suzhou City (蘇州) where he found everything had changed.

YOUTHFUL PLEASURE

Zhou Bangyan (1056 — 1121)

Glistening like water is
  the knife from Bingzhou;[1]
Whiter than snow the salt from Wu.[2]

A fresh orange you peel with your delicate hand.

The brocade bed curtain is warming up;
Smoke keeps rising
  from the beast-shape censer.

Face to face, we sit tuning the Sheng.[3]

"Where will you spend the night?"
  you whisper.
"The midnight bell on the city wall just rang.

The frost is thick and the horse may slip.
You'd do better not to go.
In the street, there's hardly any man."

---

1 Knives made in Bingzhou (并州) were famous for its sharpness. Bingzhou is now known as
 Taiyuan (太原) in Shanxi Province (山西省).

2 The area around the former Kingdom of Wu in the Zhejiang Province. Salt from Wu in the
 old days was famous for being pure, fine and snow-white. Local oranges were often sour and
 bitter in those days. Salt was therefore sprinkled before eating to enhance the taste.

3 The 'Sheng' is an old musical instrument consisting of a bundle of pipes of varying lengths
 and a bulb-shade holder.

少年遊

周邦彥 (1056 — 1121)

并刀如水，吳鹽勝雪，
　　纖手破新橙。

錦幄初溫，獸煙不斷，
　　相對坐調笙。

低聲問：向誰行宿？城上已三更。
馬滑霜濃，不如休去，直是少人行。

BUTTERFLIES IN LOVE WITH FLOWERS

Zhou Bangyan (1056 — 1121)

A bright moon startles the crows –
  they flutter with fear.

The night's ending.
Someone uses the decorated well's pulley gear,

Waking up a pair of sparkling eyes, crystal clear.
The red cotton pillow's cold with tear.

Hands grasped, in the frosty wind
  the shadows of her hair veer.

How unwilling to leave!
Parting words too sorrowful for the ear.

Upstairs, to the railing
  the Big Dipper's handle[1] moves near.
Outside in cold dew, the traveller's far away –
  only repeated calls of cocks she'd hear.

---

1 The line formed by the fifth, sixth and seventh stars of the Big Dipper (or the Plough or Northern Stars) in the sky. When the Big Dipper's handle moves near (i.e. parallel) to the balcony railing, the day is about to break.

Background:
This poem vividly describes the poet's heart-rending feelings before and during parting from his love. The veiled description of a sleepless night and a sorrowful daybreak is especially touching.

蝶戀花

周邦彥 (1056 — 1121)

月皎驚烏棲不定。
更漏將闌，轆轤牽金井。

喚起兩眸清炯炯，
淚花落枕紅棉冷。

執手霜風吹鬢影。
去意徊徨，別語愁難聽。

樓上闌干橫斗柄。
露寒人遠難相應。

JADE TOWER SPRING

Zhou Bangyan (1056 — 1121)

The peach blossom stream[1] I didn't linger around.
Autumn lotus roots were severed[2] –
    ways to re-join them can't be found.

Back then, we dated at the red-railing bridge,
Today, alone looking for her,
    for the golen-leaf path I'm bound.

In the mist, green mountain peaks abound,
The backs of wild geese
    tinted red as the sun goes down.

She, like a cloud in the wind,
    vanishes into the river;
Love, like willow catkins after the rain,
    clings to the ground.

1 The poet quoted an East Han Dynasty (A.D. 25-220) legend in which a man called Liu
  Chen and his friend met two pretty fairy girls in the remote Penglai Mountain (蓬萊山)
  and stayed happily with them for six months. When they later returned to the mountains,
  the fairy girls could not be found. Here the poet regretted he did not stay long with the girl
  he once met. She could not be traced when he later returned to the same place.

2 Connection with the girl was interrupted.

玉樓春

周邦彥 (1056 — 1121)

桃溪不作從容住，秋藕絕來無續處。
當年相候赤闌橋，今日獨尋黃葉路。

煙中列岫青無數，雁背夕陽紅欲暮。
人如風後入江雲，情似雨餘黏地絮。

MUCH ADO

An Angler's Song

Zhu Dunru (1081 — 1159)

I shook my head and
  left the material world.[1]
Sober or drunk, I simply let the time go.

I make a living in a green straw cape
  and blue bamboo hat,
Accustomed to braving the frost and snow.

The night's windless,
  my fishing line hangs idle;
A new moon's seen above and below.[2]

For a thousand miles
  the water and sky look alike,
While I watch a lone goose intermittently glow.[3]

---

1 The poet quitted his office and returned to his home village to lead a quiet life by a river as an angler.

2 The moon was reflected in the water.

3 The goose glowed now and then as it circled in and reflected the moonlight.

好事近

漁父詞

朱敦儒 (1081 — 1159)

搖首出紅塵，醒醉更無時節。
活計綠蓑青笠，慣披霜衝雪。

晚來風定釣絲閒，上下是新月。
千里水天一色，看孤鴻明滅。

RIVERBANK FAIRIES

Climbing a pavilion at night and recalling the old days in Luoyang

Chen Yuyi (1090 — 1139)

I recall drinking with friends
    on Noon Bridge[1] long ago:
Mostly heroes were they.

Down the river,
    the moon[2] was being quietly carried away.

Among the thin shadows of apricot trees,
Flutes till dawn we did play.

Twenty-odd years[3] have gone by like a dream…
Though I'd survived,
    I recall the past with dismay.

Leisurely I climbed the pavilion
    to view the night sky after a rainy day.

Many affairs of the past and present,
Would just become stories in the
    midnight fishermen's songs anyway.

---

1 Name of a famous bridge frequented by poets and dignitaries. It was located 10 *li's* (about three miles) south of Luoyang County.

2 Reflection of the moon was being carried away by the water thus alluded to the passage of time.

3 During this period, the northern territories of Song Dynasty fell into the hands of the invading Jins (金人). The poet was a court official. He escaped to the south.

臨江仙

夜登小閣憶洛中舊遊

陳與義 (1090 — 1139)

憶昔午橋橋上飲，坐中多是豪英。
長溝流月無聲。
杏花疏影裏，吹笛到天明。

二十餘年如一夢，此身雖在堪驚。
閒登小閣看新晴。
古今多少事，漁歌唱起三更。

SLOW BEAT

Li Qingzhao (1084 — 1151)

I search, I seek…
It's cold and desolate,
Dreary, miserable and bleak.

When it suddenly changes
      from warm to cold,
Hard it is to get a good rest indeed.

With a few cups of mild wine,
How can one stand
      the evening wind blowing at high speed?

A wild goose[1] passes by –
My heart breaks.
It's an old acquaintance[2] I heed.

Yellow flowers[3] pack the yard tight.
But they've withered!
Now who cares to pick them? Who might?[4]

---

1 The wild goose was a symbol of communication in ancient China. It reminded her of her old home in the north when she got news of her husband in the old days.

2 She was homesick. She seemed to recognise the wild goose which came from the north.

3 Chrysanthemums.

4 She used to pick yellow flowers in the yard with her husband who was no longer with her. The yellow flowers reminded her of the past and she was saddened.

Waiting by the window,
How can one endure the loneliness
     till arrival of the night?

The light rain beats the Wutong tree:
One by one,
Raindrops fall till twilight.

Given these conditions,
How can the word 'sorrowful' describe my plight?

Background:
The poet was the wife of a court official called Zhao Ming Cheng (趙明誠). They had a happy life before the fall of the North Song Dynasty. They escaped to the south after the northern Song territories fell into the hands of the invading Jins (金兵) in A.D. 1126. After Zhao's death in A.D. 1129, the poet lived a desolate and miserable life suffering from the loss of her country and her husband. This famous poem of hers fully reflected her sorry plight during this period.

聲聲慢

李清照 (1084 — 1151)

尋尋覓覓，
冷冷清清，淒淒慘慘戚戚。
乍暖還寒時候，最難將息。

三杯兩盞淡酒，怎敵他，晚來風急？
雁過也，正傷心，卻是舊時相識。

滿地黃花堆積，
憔悴損，如今有誰堪摘？
守着窗兒，獨自怎生得黑？

梧桐更兼細雨，到黃昏，點點滴滴。
這次第，怎一個愁字了得？

AS IN A DREAM (1)

Li Qingzhao (1084 — 1151)

Last night came scattered showers
      and a sudden strong blow.
I'm still feeling tipsy –
      had a good sleep though.

I ask my maid who's rolling up the blind,
She says no change the begonias show.

'Do you know?
Do you know?

The greens[1] have grown fat,
      the reds[2] gone thin – that would be so!'

---

1 & 2 Green leaves and red flowers of the begonia. The poet believed that after the overnight
rain and wind, the begonia leaves would have grown bigger but few flowers would have
survived. The word 'thin' in Chinese also implies 'weakness.' It was understood that she
used flowers to allude to the vulnerable fate of a woman, or herself, and felt very sad.

如夢令 (1)

李清照 (1084 — 1151)

昨夜雨疏風驟。

濃睡不消殘酒。

試問捲簾人，卻道海棠依舊。

知否？

知否？

應是綠肥紅瘦！

AS IN A DREAM (2)

Li Qingzhao (1084 — 1151)

Often I recall
    the streamside pavilion at day's end.
Dead drunk, I knew not my way home then.

Fully enjoyed,
    I turned back my boat at nightfall –
Deep into the lotus blossoms
    my way I happened to wend.

I struggled towards land,
I struggled towards land,

And startled a flock of
    gulls and egrets on the sand.

如夢令 (2)

李清照 (1084 — 1151)

常記溪亭日暮。
沉醉不知歸路。
興盡晚回舟，誤入藕花深處。

爭渡，
爭渡，
驚起一灘鷗鷺。

TIPSY UNDER THE FLOWERS

Li Qingzhao (1084 — 1151)

Light mists and thick clouds
    shroud a sorrowful never-ending day;
Camphor incense keeps rising
    from the golden beast tray.

Again, comes Chong Yang Festival[1].
By midnight, the first autumn chill
Seeps through jade pillows
    and gauze bed curtain all the way.

By the eastern hedge[2]
    I enjoy my wine after eventide,
Filling my sleeves
    with a faint fragrance[2] thereby.

I won't say I'm not grief-stricken:
The west wind's rolling up the blind,
Thinner than the yellow flower[3] am I.

---

1 The ninth day of the ninth month of the lunar calendar. People visit and pay tribute to their ancestors on this day.

2 A section of the garden where chrysanthemums were grown. Hence the fragrance of these flowers filled the poet's sleeves.

3 Chrysanthemums.

醉花陰

李清照 (1084 — 1151)

薄霧濃雲愁永晝，
瑞腦銷金獸。

佳節又重陽，玉枕紗廚，
半夜涼初透。

東籬把酒黃昏後，
有暗香盈袖。

莫道不銷魂，簾捲西風，
人比黃花瘦。

HEAVENLY BARBARIAN

Li Qingzhao (1084 — 1151)

The breeze is gentle,
> the sun mild in early spring.
Just put on, a cheerful mood
> the lined coat seems to bring.

A bit chilly is felt on getting up;
The plum blossom
> on my temple[1] has dried up.

Where's the old home of mine?
Would forget it only when drunk on wine.

The eaglewood incense[2]
> was lit before going to bed;
Gone is its scent but
> tipsy I still feel in my head.

---

1 The poet probably slept with the plum blossom on her temple the night before when she was drunk.

2 Eaglewood (沉香 / 沉水) has a very high density. It sinks in water. Its chips were used as incense in the old days and were burnt to produce a fragrant smoke.

菩薩蠻

李清照 (1084 — 1151)

風柔日薄春猶早，夾衫乍著心情好。
　睡起覺微寒，梅花鬢上殘。

　故鄉何處是？忘了除非醉。
　沈水臥時燒，香消酒未消。

SPRING AT WULING

Li Qingzhao (1084 — 1151)

The wind has subsided, sweet dust lingers
    but the flowers have withered.
I'm weary of combing my hair
    as the sun hangs low.

Things remain but he's gone[1]–
    and with him all will go…
Before I can speak, tears flow.

Upon hearing
    spring's still fair in the Twin Brooks[2],
A light boat I'd like to row.

But I fear the Twin Brooks' grasshopper-boat[3],
Couldn't carry,
So much woe.

---

1 The poet and her husband both love poetry and had a happy life in harmonious partnership. The poet's husband had an early deathsome ten years after they were married and she was left in lonely widowhood.

2 Name of a river in a scenic place in Jin Hua (金華), Zhejiang Province where she had some good time with her husband before.

3 A small boat shaped like a grasshopper.

武陵春

李清照 (1084 — 1151)

風住塵香花已盡，日晚倦梳頭。
物是人非事事休，欲語淚先流。

聞說雙溪春尚好，也擬泛輕舟。
只恐雙溪舴艋舟，載不動，許多愁。

THE RIVER RUNS RED

Yue Fei (1103 — 1142)

My hair bristles with rage, thrusting at my helmet.
By the balustrade,
The pattering rain is gone.

Lifting my eyes,
I give a long roar into the sky:
My young heart's burning with a desire so strong.

At thirty[1], honour to me is like dust and earth;
Across eight thousand *li's*[2],
      under the clouds and moon[3] we fight on.

Idle not:
A young man's hair soon turns grey –
Vainly one'd mourn.

---

1 Yue Fei wrote this great poem in A.D. 1134 at the height of his military career at the age of 31.

2 One Chinese *li* equals about 0.3 mile.

3 This indicates that the poet and his troop had been fighting non-stop day and night across thousands of miles against the Tartars or Jins (金人) in an effort to recover lost territories.

4 In the second year of Jing Kang (宋欽宗靖康二年) (A.D. 1127), the Song capital fell into the hands of the invading Jins (金人). Both Emperor Hui and Emperor Qin (徽、欽二帝) were abducted and taken to the north. This was considered to be a huge shame for the nation.

5 Mt. Helan is a large mountain lying between China and Mongolia. The stronghold of the Tartars at the time was in the mountain pass.

The shame of Jing Kang[4],
Still hasn't been wiped away;

The grudge we bear as subjects –
When will it be erased, say?

We'd ride long chariots
To smash Mt. Helan Pass[5] all the way.

When hungry,
　　with resolution, the Tartars' flesh eat we'd;
When thirsty,
　　with jokes, their blood drink we may.

Let me start afresh,
To recover the lost territories
And present our victory
　　to the Emperor on audience day.

Background:
Yue Fei, a legendary patriot in Song Dynasty, joined the army at the age of 19 and spent his entire short life fighting the invading Jins (金兵). A great warfare talent, he soon became the most successful commander who had won battles after battles against the Jins. He established his own Yue's Troop (岳家軍) which was so powerful that the Jins had great dread upon hearing the name. Unfortunately, he was vilified, recalled to the capital and executed for treason in 1142 at the age of 39. He was later rehabilitated by a decree of Emperor Song Xiaozong (宋孝宗 1163-1189).

滿江紅

岳飛 (1103 — 1142)

怒髮衝冠，憑闌處、瀟瀟雨歇。
抬望眼、仰天長嘯，壯懷激烈。

三十功名塵與土，八千里路雲和月。
莫等閒、白了少年頭，空悲切。

靖康恥，猶未雪。
臣子恨，何時滅？
駕長車踏破，賀蘭山缺。

壯志飢餐胡虜肉，笑談渴飲匈奴血。
待從頭、收拾舊山河，朝天闕。

PHOENIX HAIRPIN

Lu You (1125 — 1210)

Hands pink and fine;
Yellow-seal wine[1].
Spring's colours fill the town but the willow's[2]
    trapped within the palace confines.

The east wind[3] was overly strong:
Our happiness didn't last long.

Separated for years,
A gloomy spirit all along.
Wrong! Wrong! Wrong!

Spring's the same as previous years,
But haggard your face appears:
Your silk handkerchief soaked with rouged tears[4].

---

1 Precious fine wine in delicate jars bearing a yellowish royal seal.

2 The poet alluded to his wife who was now in another man's arms just like the willow that was confined within the palace walls.

3 The east wind was blamed for blowing off flowers. Here the poet alluded to his mother who forced him to divorce his wife.

4 Tears mixed with rouge. Rouge is a red cosmetic powder used by women as make-up in the old days.

Peach petals fall;
Desolate the ponds and pavilions grow.

Our oath of love firm as ever,
But brocade letters to you would never go.
No! No! No!

Background:

This poem recorded a famous love tragedy in the Southern Song Dynasty. Lu You (1125-1210) was a famous patriotic poet. He and his wife Tang Wan (唐琬), who was also a distinguished poet, were deeply in love. Unfortunately, Tang was not acceptable to Lu's mother. Lu divorced Tang on instruction of his mother.

They met again on a fine spring day nine years afterwards in Shen's Garden (沈 園). Tang was touring the garden with her second husband with whose approval, Tang entertained Lu with fine yellow-seal official wine. In return, Lu wrote the above lyric on the garden wall. Tang replied with another equally if not more touching lyric poem of the same tune. Tang died of a broken heart not long thereafter. See Tang's poem immediately following Lu You's poems.

釵頭鳳

陸游 (1125 — 1210)

紅酥手，黃縢酒，
滿城春色宮牆柳。

東風惡，歡情薄，
一懷愁緒，幾年離索。錯！錯！錯！

春如舊，人空瘦，
淚痕紅浥鮫綃透。

桃花落，閒池閣。
山盟雖在，錦書難托。莫！莫！莫！

SPRING AT XIE'S POOL

Lu You (1125 — 1210)

I joined the military in my prime,
And determined to gobble up
    the Tartars with all my might.

High were the serried clouds,
Beacon fires flared in the night.

Ruddy-cheeked and black-haired,
Carved spear in hand on the western battle site.

How laughable, scholars[1] were often wrong
    when looking back in hindsight.

I roam about Wu and Chu[2] in a skiff,
Dreams of honour shattered despite.

Sad songs I sing at will,
Lamenting the past in a sorry plight.

Beyond boundless mist and waves,
The Chin Pass[3] is out of sight!

Alas, I've wasted the passing years outright!

1 Scholars attached to the troops were often open to ridicule on their ability in military affairs. The poet was one of such scholars. It is believed that he was probably reflecting on himself.

2 Wu and Chu referred to places in River South. Here it meant places around the home of the poet in Shaoxing, Zhejiang Province (浙江省紹興市).

3 A battle site in which the poet once stationed at the frontier in Han Zhong, Shaanxi Province (陝西省漢中地區).

謝池春

陸游 (1125 — 1210)

壯歲從戎，曾是氣吞殘虜。
陣雲高，狼煙夜舉。

朱顏青鬢，擁雕戈西戍。
笑儒冠自來多誤。

功名夢斷，卻泛扁舟吳楚。
漫悲歌，傷懷弔古。

煙波無際，望秦關何處？
歎流年又成虛度。

Background:
The poet joined the military in A.D. 1172 at the age of 48 at a time when the Song Empire was truncated after the North Provinces were lost to the invading Jurgens i.e. the Jins (金人). He had high ambitions and was well-known as a patriotic poet. He advocated launching a full-scale battle to recapture the North but his proposition was not accepted. This poem was written at home after his retirement. His dream of doing something great for his country was never realized.

THE DIVINER

Song of the Plum

Lu You (1125 — 1210)

By a broken bridge outside a courier post,
In loneliness it blooms, free from rein.

Alone, laden with sorrow at dusk,
And battered by the wind and rain.

Vie bitterly for springtime glories it'd not;
Allow the jealousy of other flowers it'd fain.

When fallen, its blossoms would become mud
    and crushed into dust[1]–
Only their fragrance would remain.

---

1 After they were run over by the couriers' carriages.

卜算子

詠梅

陸游 (1125 — 1210)

驛外斷橋邊，寂寞開無主。
已是黃昏獨自愁，
更著風和雨。

無意苦爭春，一任羣芳妒。
零落成泥碾作塵，
只有香如故。

Background:
The poet used the fate of plum blossoms as an allusion to his unswerving integrity in the face of jealousy and vilification.

NIGHT REVELS IN THE PALACE

To Shi Bohun after Recalling a Dream

Lu You (1125 — 1210)

Bugles blared all over at the break of a snowy day;
In my dream, I roamed –
Not knowing into where did I stray.

Like flowing water, noiselessly
    advanced the cavalry in battle array.

I recalled the frontier passes and rivers[1]
Bordering Qinghai[2],
West of the Yan Men Gateway[3].

To the cold light of the lamp I awake:
The water clock has ceased dripping,
Through the window comes the slanting moon ray.

1, 2 & 3 Places in the ancient north-east frontier near Qinghai Lake in Qinghai Province west
of Yan Men Gateway in Shanxi Province (山西雁門關) where fierce battles were fought
between the Tang army and the invading Jins (金人).

4 It was a tradition in ancient China for the Emperor to confer grants and honour to the army
leader upon his winning a major battle at the frontier.

I long to become a nobleman by
    imperial grant ten thousand miles away[4].

Who'd know?
My heart isn't dead,
Though my temples have turned grey.

Background:
This poem was written possibly between A.D. 1174 to 1177. The poet started serving in the army from A.D. 1172. He had always longed to make great contribution to his country so as to become a nobleman by imperial grant. Unfortunately, his wishes were not realized. The last stanza of the poem indicated that he was still hoping to achieve his goal.

夜遊宮

記夢，寄師伯渾

陸游 (1125 — 1210)

雪曉清笳亂起，
夢遊處，不知何地？
鐵騎無聲似水。

想關河，雁門西，
青海際。

睡覺寒燈裏，
漏聲斷，月斜窗紙。
自許封侯在萬里。

有誰知？鬢雖殘，
心未死。

PARTRIDGE WEATHER

Lu You (1125 — 1210)

Amid mists and the setting sun's glow,
    my home I find;
I'm not at all concerned
    about worldly affairs of any kind.

I thread through the bamboos after
    pouring fine wine to the last cup;
I lie down to watch the hills after
    enjoying Huangting[1] to the last line.

A carefree life I love –
No matter how my health has declined.
Offering a smiling face
    wherever I'm I won't mind.

I should have known
    the Creator[2] had other ideas –
An old hero is simply left behind.

---

1 The Book of Huangting (黃庭經), a classical Daoist book on how to keep good health.
2 He in fact alluded to the Emperor of South Song Dynasty. He avoided using the word 'Emperor'.

鷓鴣天

陸游 (1125 — 1210)

家住蒼煙落照間，絲毫塵事不相關。
斟殘玉瀣行穿竹，卷罷黃庭臥看山。

貪嘯傲，任衰殘。不妨隨處一開顏。
元知造物心腸別，老卻英雄似等閒。

Background:
This poem was written in A.D. 1166 when the poet lived by the Mirror Lake in Zhejiang Province. He was unhappy as the South Song Emperor had no intention to launch a fight-back to recapture the northern provinces which were lost to the invading Jurgens i.e. the Jins (金人). Many patriots like him were being left idle and disappointed.

PHOENIX HAIRPIN

Tang Wan (Date of birth and death unknown)

The world's unkind;
People have an evil mind.

Dusk has gone with the rain,
  leaving fallen blossoms behind.

The morning wind dried my tears
And left a faint mark.

I wish to write –
Alone by the slanting railing, I lay bare my heart.
Hard! Hard! Hard!

We're on different ways;
Gone are our days.

Like the ropes of a swing,
  my ailing spirit often sways.

The horn[1] chills my mind;
The night has declined.

For fear of being questioned,
I hold back tears to look gratified.
Hide! Hide! Hide!

---

1 A horn was brown at night to signal time in ancient days.

釵頭鳳

唐琬（生卒年不詳）

世情薄，人情惡，
雨送黃昏花易落。

曉風乾，淚痕殘。
欲箋心事，獨語斜闌。難！難！難！

人成各，今非昨，
病魂常似秋千索。

角聲寒，夜闌珊。
怕人尋問，咽淚妝歡。瞞！瞞！瞞！

Background:
This lyric poem was written on the wall in Shen's Garden in reply to a similar poem written by her former husband, Lu You (陸游). She died of a broken heart not long thereafter.

BREAKING THROUGH THE RANKS

To Chen Tongfu

Xin Qiji (1140 — 1207)

While drunk, I trim[1] the lamp
　　and gaze at my sword.
Awaken from a dream to the camps,
　　I still hear the battle horns sound…

Roasted beef[2] being distributed to soldiers;
Fifty-string zithers
　　　　playing tunes only in frontiers found[3];

Troops being mustered
　　　　in the autumn battleground.

Horses fast as Dilo[4],
Bowstrings emitting
　　　　shocking, thunderous sound.

One'd strive to achieve the Emperor's goal[5],
So that before and after death,
　　　　one'd become renowned.

What a pity, grey hairs on my head abound!

1　He trimmed the wick of the lamp to make it burn brighter.

2　(八百里) is an ancient name in the military for beef.

3　Battle tunes played only in the frontiers.

4　Name of a famous, extremely fast horse that belonged to Liu Bei (劉備) in the Three Kingdoms Period (三國時期). It took Liu to safety with its extreme speed during a narrow escape from the enemies.

5　Recovery of the northern provinces lost to the Jins (金人).

破陣子

為陳同父賦壯語以寄

辛棄疾 (1140 — 1207)

醉裏挑燈看劍，夢回吹角連營。

八百里分麾下炙，
五十弦翻塞外聲，
沙場秋點兵。

馬作的盧飛快，弓如霹靂弦驚。

了卻君王天下事，
贏得生前身後名，
可憐白髮生。

Background:
Xin Qiji, a well-known patriot who was born not long after the northern provinces of Song (宋) were taken by the invading Jins (女真族). Determined to wipe away the national shame, he led a troop of 3,000 volunteers to assist the Court in battles. However, his later petition to launch large-scale fight-back to recover the northern territories was not accepted by the South Song Emperor. He was vilified and sacked. In this poem, the poet vividly recalled and recorded his military life in the frontiers and his deep regret at his failure to fulfil his ambition before becoming old.

GREEN JADE BOWL

Lantern Festival Night

Xin Qiji (1140 — 1207)

The east wind unfolded blossoms[1]
    on thousands of trees that night;
It blew apart the fireworks[2]
That rained down like stars twinkling bright.

Noble horses, carved carriages and
    perfumed revellers packed the road tight.

Phoenix flutes resounding all over;
Jade lanterns flashing and revolving;
Fish and dragon lanterns dancing all night.

With paper moths, paper flowers and
    gold-threaded hairpins[3] the girls bedight;
Leaving behind a faint fragrance,
    they laughed and chatted along in delight.

Thousands of times I searched for her
    among the crowds but she wasn't in sight.

Suddenly, as I turned my head –
There she was,
In the dim, fading lantern light.

1 There were so many colourful lanterns hanging on trees that it was like thousands of trees blossoming in the east wind (i.e. the spring wind).
2 Researches indicated that fireworks were played at this important festival in the Song Dynasty.
3 These were favourite ornaments worn by ladies on their hair during important festivals in the Song Dynasty.

青玉案

元夕

辛棄疾 (1140 — 1207)

東風夜放花千樹，
更吹落，星如雨。

寶馬雕車香滿路。
鳳簫聲動，玉壺光轉，一夜魚龍舞。

娥兒雪柳黃金縷，
笑語盈盈暗香去。

眾裏尋他千百度。
驀然回首，那人卻在，燈火闌珊處。

Background:
The poet described the scene as he saw it and how he eventually found 'her' on Lantern Festival night (on the fifteenth day of the first month or the first full moon of the year) in Lin An (臨安), the capital of South Song Dynasty (i.e. today's Hangzhou City, Zhejiang Province) in A.D. 1170.

HEAVENLY BARBARIAN

(Written on the Wall at Zaokou in Jiangxi Province)

Xin Qiji (1140 — 1207)

Below Yu Ku Terrace[1],
  the Qing Jiang[2] River flows.
How many travellers
  had shed tears in it[3] no one knows.

I look towards Chang An[4] in the north-west,
What a pity,
  before me are countless mountain crests.

The blue mountains can't stop its flow:
After all, eastwards the river continues to go.

By the river, I am saddened at nightfall;
Deep in the woods, I hear the partridges call[5].

1 An ancient and historic raised terrace by the side of the Qing Jiang River.

2 The section where the Yuan River (袁水) meets the Kong River (贛水) in the southeast of Kongzhou (贛州 in Jiangxi Province) was formerly called Qing Jiang River.

3 Thousands of innocent people were killed in this area by the invading Jurchens (女真族即 金兵) in 1129.

4 Capital of Song Dynasty. It is in today's Xian (西安).

5 Partridges make distinctive sad six-note calls sounding like "you can go nowhere" in Chinese (行不得也哥哥).

菩薩蠻

書江西省造口壁

辛棄疾 (1140 — 1207)

鬱孤臺下清江水。中間多少行人淚。
西北望長安。可憐無數山。

青山遮不住。畢竟東流去。
江晚正愁予。山深聞鷓鴣。

PURE SERENE MUSIC

A night spent alone in Wang's Monastery in Bo Shan

Xin Qiji (1140 — 1207)

Circling my bed is a hungry rat;
Dancing around the lamp a bat.

Above the house, winds from the pines
       drive the rain mad;
Broken paper window panes
       among themselves chat.

In northern frontiers and
       south of Yangtze, all my life I spent,
Upon return, white-haired
       and weather-beaten I stand.

Awaken from an autumn night dream
       under a cotton quilt,
Before my eyes are
       ten thousand miles of national land.

Background:
The poet spent a night inside a more or less deserted monastery after his retirement between A.D. 1182-1187. Awaken from a dream, he felt sad that the large swathe of national land lost to the Jins (金人) was still not recaptured.

清平樂

獨宿博山王氏庵

辛棄疾 (1140 — 1207)

繞床飢鼠，蝙蝠翻燈舞。
屋上松風吹急雨，破紙窗間自語。

平生塞北江南，歸來華髮蒼顏。
布被秋宵夢覺，眼前萬里江山。

UGLY SLAVE

Xin Qiji (1140 — 1207)

In youth, I knew not the taste of sorrow:
Upstairs I loved to climb.

Upstairs I loved to climb,
And made up sorrowful phrases
        for the sake of a new rhyme.

Now I know all about the taste of sorrow,
I hesitate to speak my mind.

I hesitate to speak my mind,
Instead, I say autumn days are cool and fine.

醜奴兒

辛棄疾 (1140 — 1207)

少年不識愁茲味，愛上層樓。
愛上層樓，為賦新詞強說愁。

而今識盡愁茲味，欲說還休。
欲說還休，欲道天涼好個秋。

WEST RIVER MOON

Seeking Relief from Boredom

Xin Qiji (1140 — 1207)

Joy is what I crave for when drunk;
Sorrow surely has no part to play.

I find of late
That ancient writings
aren't trustworthy in any way.

Last night I lay drunk beside a pine tree.
I asked it, 'how drunk am I would you say?'

Suspecting it was about
to help as it seemed to sway,
I pushed it saying, 'go away!'

西江月

遣興

辛棄疾 (1140 — 1207)

醉裏且貪歡笑，要愁那得功夫。
近來始覺古人書，
信著全無是處。

昨夜松邊醉倒，問松：我醉何如？
只疑松動要來扶，
以手推松曰：去！

THE DIVINER

Song of the Begonia

Liu Ke Zhuang (1187 — 1269)

Like the wings of butterflies,
    their petals are flimsy;
Like scattered scarlet dots,
    their flowers are few.

If Heaven doesn't cherish flowers,
Why, in their countless varieties,
    they all look so cute?

At daybreak, they flourish on tree tops;
By dusk, what remain on the boughs are few.

If Heaven does cherish flowers,
Why then, the wind and rain
    they can't pull through?

卜算子

詠海棠

劉克莊 (1187 — 1269)

片片蝶衣輕，點點猩紅少。
道是天公不惜花，百種千般巧。

朝見樹頭繁，暮見枝頭少。
道是天公果惜花，雨洗風吹了。

PURE SERENE MUSIC

Playing with the moon on the 15th night of the 5th month

Liu Kezhuang (1187 — 1269)

The waves rolled fast as the wind rose high;
Through ten thousand miles
    on the back of the toad[1] I did ride.

The real demeanour of Chang E[2] I've eyed:
Her face had no make-up applied.

The palace of silver and pearls[3] I toured around,
But it was hazy all over as I looked down.

In drunkenness,
    by chance I shook the laurel tree[4],
Making what men called breezes on the ground.

1 Ancient legend says a toad lives on the moon. The poet was drunk, he imagined he rode ten thousand miles on the back of the toad and landed on the moon.

2 A pretty lady who lives on the moon according to the legend.

3 The palace which was believed to be on the moon.

4 A five-thousand-feet high laurel tree grows on the moon according to the legend.

清平樂

五月十五夜玩月

劉克莊 (1187 — 1269)

風高浪快，萬里騎蟾背。
曾識姮娥真體態，素面原無粉黛。

身遊銀闕珠宮，俯看積氣濛濛。
醉裏偶搖桂樹，人間喚作涼風。

SANDS AT SILK-WASHING STREAM

Wu Wenying (c1200 — c1260)

I dreamt I went to our old meeting-place
  but flowers were dense, doors shut tight.
In the wordless sunset, a swallow[1]
  was left to grieve after its return flight.

Around a small curtain hook,
  delicate, fragrant hands were in sight[2].

Willow flowers fall in silence –
  spring's shedding tears[3];
Drifting clouds cast shadows –
  the moon's hidden from sight[4].

The east wind's colder than autumn by night.

1　An allusion. The poet himself was left to grieve.

2　The poet dreamt that he went to the house where he used to have meetings with his lover but was unable to enter because the doors were shut tight. In despair, he imagined seeing his lover unrolling the curtain inside the house with her delicate hands as she did in the old days.

3　Upon waking up from his dream, the poet was saddened when he saw willow catkins falling, which reminded him of his lover crying at the time of their parting.

4　This line alluded to the shy look of the poet's lover before they parted.

浣溪沙

吳文英 (約 1200 — 1260)

門隔花深夢舊遊，夕陽無語燕歸愁。
玉纖香動小簾鉤。

落絮無聲春墮淚，行雲有影月含羞。
東風臨夜冷於秋。

THE DIVINER

Shi Xiaoyou (Date of birth and death unknown)

Why did we meet so late?
Why does parting come right away?

Hard it is to part from you –
    hard as well to be re-united.
No basis to believe meet again we may.

How can I leave, if I must leave?
How can I stay, if I want to stay?

Hard it is to stay – hard as well to leave.
Now it's hard to find a way.

卜算子

石孝友（生卒年不詳）

見也如何暮？別也如何遽？
別也應難見也難，後會難憑據。

去也如何去？住也如何住？
住也應難去也難，此際難分付。

FAIR LADY YU

Jiang Jie (Around 13th century)

I listened to the rain
in sing-song houses when I was young.
The red candlelight was dim,
the bed curtain lowly hung.

In my prime inside guest boats,
I listened to the rain.
Low were the clouds above a wide river;
Crying in the west wind was a strayed crane[1].

Now I listen to the rain
while in a monk's hut I stay –
My hair has already turned grey.

Joys and sorrows, meetings and partings
come heartlessly off and on…
Oh, let the rain drip on the steps till dawn.

---

1 The poet passed the State Examination at the age of 30 in A.D. 1276. Song Dynasty was toppled three year later. He refused to serve the new Court, left his home and wandered about in the South. Hence, he felt he was like a strayed crane that had lost its home and companions.

虞美人

蔣捷（約13世紀）

少年聽雨歌樓上，
　紅燭昏羅帳。

壯年聽雨客舟中，
江闊雲低，斷雁叫秋風。

而今聽雨僧廬下，
　鬢已星星也。

悲歡離合總無情，
一任階前滴到明。

PURE SERENE MUSIC

Zhang Yan (1240 — 1320?)

No flower-picking girls could be seen.
Suddenly I was in no mood
for sightseeing as I had been.

A guest preoccupied by poetic sorrows,
I just took a cursory look at the spring scene.

Last year, to the sky's end the swallow[1] had flown;
This year, where's the swallow's home?

Listen not to the night rain in the third month,
Now it doesn't hasten flowers to bloom[2].

1 The poet himself.
2 The poet was feeling very sad. He thought the spring rain won't bring flowers though
   normally it would.

清平樂

張炎 (1240 — 1320?)

采芳人杳，頓覺遊情少。
客裏看春多草草，總被詩愁分了。

去年燕子天涯，今年燕子誰家。
三月休聽夜雨，如今不是催花。

Background:
The capital of South Song, Lin An (臨安) (today's Hang Zhou (杭州)), fell into the hands of Mongolian troops in A.D. 1276. The poet's properties were confiscated and members of his family killed. He escaped to far-off places. This poem was written when he returned to Hang Zhou after many years and paid a visit to the West Lake (西湖). He was sad to find the place which used to be rather crowded had become desolate.

THE WILLOW TIPS ARE GREEN

Thoughts in Spring

Liu Chengweng (1232 — 1297)

War horses in Mongolian blankets;
Silvery fireworks sprinkling down tears.
Spring comes to the sorrowful town.

Flutes playing barbarian tunes;
Actors performing barbarian street mimes.
They aren't musical sound.

How unbearable
　　　　sitting alone by the green lamp!
I miss my homeland and
The bright moon above the mound.

Scenes in the capital!
My time in the hills!
My heart's now sea-bound².

1　See last sentence in 'Background'.

Background:
This poem depicts the tragic scene on the night of the Lantern Festival, i.e. the first full moon night of the year (元宵節) in the capital Lin An (臨安) under Mongolian occupation in A.D. 1277 soon after the fall of the Southern Song Empire. The poet was taking refuge in the desolate hills near his native village in Jiangxi Province. He once served under the legendary Wen Tianxiang (文天祥 1236-1283) and was greatly saddened being unable to contribute to his homeland. His heart was tied to the patriots led by Lu Xiufu (陸秀夫) and others who escaped by sea to the southern coastal areas of Guangdong and Fujian Provinces trying hard to re-establish the fallen Empire.

柳梢青

春感

劉辰翁 (1232 — 1297)

鐵馬蒙氈，銀花灑淚，春入愁城。
笛裏番腔，街頭戲鼓，不是歌聲。

那堪獨坐青燈。想故國，高台月明。
輦下風光，山中歲月，海上心情。

Bibliography
參考書目

(1) *A Book of Chinese Verse* by R. H. Kotewall & N. L. Smith, The Hong Kong University Press, 1990.

(2) *A Golden Treasury of Chinese Poetry* by John A. turner, The Chinese University Press, Hong Kong, 1989.

(3) *A Silver Treasury of Chinese Lyrics*, Edited by Alice W. Cheng, The Chinese University Press, Hong Kong, 2003.

(4) *Chinese Love Poetry*, Edited by Jane Portal, British Museum Press, U.K., 2004.

(5) *Song Without Music*, Chinese Tz'u Poetry, Edited by Stephen C. Soong, The Chinese University Press, Hong Kong, 1980.

(6) *A Brotherhood in Song, Chinese Poetry and Poetics*, Edited by Stephen C. Soong, The Chinese University Press, Hong Kong, 1985.

(7) *The Four Seasons of Tang Poetry* by John C. H. Wu, Charles E. Tuttle Company, Inc. of Rutland, Vermont & Tokyo Japan, 1972.

(8) *An Anthology of Chinese Literature, Beginning to 1911* by Stephen Owen, W.W. Norton & Company, New York and London, 1996.

(1) 《唐宋詞三百首》，名家配畫誦讀本，香港商務印書館出版，2000年。

(2) 《新譯宋詞三百首》，汪中注釋，臺灣三民書局印行，1977年11月。

(3) 《中國文學史》，韓高年編著，台灣聯經出版事業股份有限公司。

(4) 《唐宋名家詞選》，龍沐勛編選，卓清芬注說，臺灣里仁書局發行，2007年。

(5) 《唐宋名家詞選》，龍沐勛編選，香港商務印書館出版，1960年。

(6) 《唐宋詞格律》，龍榆生著，上海古籍出版社，2010年3月。

(7) 《人間詞話》，王國維著，徐調孚校註，香港中和出版有限公司2016年6月。

(8) 《宋詞三百首簡注》，注者：武玉成、顧叢龍，三聯書店（香港）有限公司，2002年8月。

(9) 《中華文化百家書・宋詞》，主編：遲乃義、鉑淳，三聯書店（香港）有限公司，2014年12月。

(10) 《唐宋詞鑒賞》，李永田，香港商務印書館出版，2011年。

(11) 《宋詞三百首》，康震、向鐵生注譯，中華書局（香港）有限公司，2012年12月。